Stark Choices

Peter Carroll

Raven Crest Books

ISBN-13: 978-0-9926700-2-3

ISBN-10: 0-99-267002-0

For Sharon and Megan

1. GOING UNDERGROUND

Sweat rolled off him. Darkness enveloping, trees creaking in the breeze. Every rustle and squeak from the undergrowth seemingly taking place within millimetres of his ears. Signals raced along nerves with far more vigour and regularity than normal. Surely, at some point, he'd run out of adrenalin.

Who would have known digging a grave could be such hard work? Mind you, a decent spade would have made life a lot easier.

This was a nightmare, so not part of the plan. It made things far more complicated, made getting the money even more important. Fantasies about sun-drenched beaches with palm trees, far from the reach of prosecuting authorities, danced through his mind. They needed to. He wouldn't entertain the alternative.

The hole might be big enough but, as he'd never dug one for this purpose before, he couldn't be certain. More worrying was whether or not this spot was sufficiently secluded for his needs. Would it remain undetected long enough for the money to afford him a getaway. You read in the papers about dog walkers and other nosey bastards discovering murderer's handiwork while "out walking in the countryside". He qualified as a murderer now, hoped it would take more than a casual stroll or a sniffing dog to uncover his handiwork.

He stopped, heart crashing against ribcage in violent

protest at the strain it was being put under. Sitting down, he lit a cigarette, putting yet more stress on his physiology as he tried to recover some composure. He looked down at his soiled clothes and filthy hands, wished he'd decided on burning or dumping at sea. The other thing he remembered from newspapers and TV was how tiny fragments of dirt can be traced back to specific areas, how even scrubbing yourself doesn't remove all the particles that might leave a breadcrumb trail for the police. Too late now, he was committed. The longer he took to sort this, the more likely it wouldn't end well for him.

The monumental scale of this fuck up couldn't be avoided. His brother would be furious; always chiding him for his temper, telling him to show more restraint. Should he even tell his brother? Maybe he could keep it quiet. No, his brother was way smarter, the clever one. He'd know something was amiss, and the threat of discovery would be hanging over him if he stayed around. Too much, too stressful, waiting to get caught. If he ran, his brother would need to know why. He'd need his help.

But it wasn't his fault. He never meant to kill anyone. An accident, a reflex borne out of innumerable similar encounters, only more violent, more final than the others. Lucky and unlucky in equal measure.

Was that rain? Oh, good. Just what he needed. Yes, there you go; a few drips, now a steady stream of droplets cascading down. Sure, soft ground, easier to dig, but Christ, he was going to get filthier than ever.

He stood up, flicked his cigarette butt into the hole and got back to digging. The sooner this was over with the better.

2. LOSERS AND WINNERS

"Hang on...can't be...is that...Billy!"

No response.

"Oh my God, oh my God. Billy! Get in here the now, I need you to check these numbers for me."

Still nothing.

Stella's fingers shook. Eyes flicked from television screen to ticket: tantalising bearer of pink, paper promises. Promises made but never kept – until now.

"Ten, aye, fourteen, aye, thirty-four, aye, thirty-five, aye, forty, aye, forty-nine..."

The last aye would not leave her lips. It couldn't be right. It just couldn't be. People like her didn't win the lottery. She was a loser; always had been always would be. This was a cruel trick, a dream maybe, perhaps a spiked drink, but definitely a mistake. The numbers taunted her – held in suspended animation by the satellite box. They couldn't afford satellite television but they got it anyway. Billy spent most of his waking hours in front of the television, watching football and any other manner of crap it spewed forth, balancing a can of Stella (the irony was never lost on her) on his sizeable gut, as he took root in the couch. Typically, now she actually needed him to be doing just that, he'd pulled a Lord Lucan on her.

"Billy!"she roared.

Nothing. Where was he? No chance the kids would be around, so she was on her own it seemed.

"Ten, aye, fourteen, aye, thirty-four, aye, thirty-five, aye, forty, aye, forty-nine..."

The last aye refused to join the others again. Stubborn little bastard, forcing her to doubt her sanity. But, she couldn't have won. She absolutely could not have won the sodding lottery. It was impossible. The odds were ridiculous. She was ridiculous. She must have made a mistake.

Six little numbers in ascending order. Printed in black on pink. Fingers crossed.

"Ten, aye, fourteen, aye, thirty-four, aye, thirty-five, aye, forty, aye, forty-nine..."

Say it! Say aye! The voice in her head wailed like a factory siren. Stella could feel her heart racing, the prickle of sweat, the heat of something much more significant than an early-onset menopausal flush. Fumbling for her mobile, she punched in her sister's details.

"Hiya, Stella. How are you, doll?"

Her throat felt as if someone was slowly wrapping a coil of barbed wire around the inside of it.

"Stella? You alright, hen?"

"Aye."

Finally, the wee bugger made an appearance. Not quite where she needed it, but it was a start.

"Maureen, have you seen the lottery the night?"

Everyone else called her little sister Mo but Stella didn't like to use this abbreviation. Sounded too much like a cartoon character or that dopey woman that used to be on Eastenders for her liking.

"Aye, for all the bloody good it did me. Two numbers as usual, do not pass go, do not collect ten quid, never mind the jackpot!" A cackle rasped and wheezed out of her sister, betraying a problematic fondness for tobacco and alcohol.

"Have you got it up on your satellite box?"

"Naw, I told you I didn't win anything, so why would I? What's going on, Stella?"

"I, I think...I think I've won it."

There was no conviction in her voice, no delight, no celebration. She hoped this might make it more plausible.

"Oh aye, that's right, you've won the fuckin lottery! And I'm shagging Simon Cowell! Away you go, it's no April the first is it?" The cackle crackled with increased vigour.

"Seriously, Maureen, I think I've won it. Please check the numbers on the telly for me so I can make sure I've no' made a total arse of it and got mixed up!"

This time urgency, fear and sincerity.

"Holy shit! Really? You're no' just winding me up, Stella?"

"No! Please, Maureen, I need you to check these numbers!"

"But, where's Billy, can he no' check for you?"

"I've no idea where he is or where either of the boys are. That's why I'm on the phone to you."

"Right, ok. Wait the now, I need to sort the telly out."

A pause. A muffled argument with her daughter about interrupting her evening's viewing, followed by incredulous, expletive-strewn accession. More profanities regarding how the box worked.

"Right, Stella. I'm back, doll." Stella was unaccustomed to hearing her normally cocksure sister's voice quivering with nervousness. "Read out your numbers."

"Ok. Just to check first. It is Saturday right?"

The cackle ripped through their tension like a chainsaw.

"You daft cow, of course it's Saturday!"

"Aye, ok, ok, just checking. I'm so nervous Maureen, I can hardly stand up or hold this phone. What if I have won it? It's millions. No' a tenner or a couple of grand...millions!"

"I know that, Stella! But, we'll never know if you've won it or no' if you don't read out the bloody numbers. Hurry up, before I take a coronary!"

Stella realised her vision was blurring and someone

must have opened a secret door to a nearby blast furnace because she was on fire, sweat lashing off her.

"Right, here goes. Ten?"

"Aye."

"Fourteen?"

"Aye."

"Thirty-four?"

"Aye, so that's the tenner then!"

"Shoosh, Maureen, for Christ's sake!"

"Alright, keep your bloody hair on! Next?"

"Thirty-five?"

"Aye."

"Forty?"

"Aye. Sweet baby Jesus woman, you better no' be on the wind-up here!"

"Mo, for fuck's sake will you let me read out these numbers!"

The words flew from her as if fired from an automatic weapon. Her sister felt wounded by their ferocity and the uncharacteristic abbreviation of her name.

"Forty-nine?"

The scream, tumult and incoherent babbling that ensued confirmed what Stella had known for the last thirty minutes. Things were never going to be the same again.

Aye.

3. HOME SWEET HOME

Paris, Milan, New York, London...Alloa.

Adam Stark sat in his car watching the lads playing football in the drizzle. The drive through the scheme of his youth, the Bottom End, or Mar Policies to give it its formal name, was a spontaneous, unplanned jaunt into his history. A strange and rather pointless thing to be doing considering he'd moved back to the area permanently and could rely on seeing plenty of action around these parts in due course. Still.

Judging ages was never a forte but the lads in question were pre-teen and probably older than seven. Twenty-odd headless chickens, with a long way to go before they understood game plans, tactics or formations. He remembered when sports were that simple for him too. Unbridled joy, unfettered by the anxiety of the consequence of failure. He remembered a time when life in general was like that. It was just a strange notion now, as if it never really happened to him.

The meeting with DCI Morris Hargreaves in London went as expected. The boss brought all his favourite characters with him: condescension sneered, smugness and told-you-so bounced up and down in their seat, disapproval sat and shook his head, but surprise, surprise, gratitude failed to put in an appearance. Stark took it on the chin and walked away from a career in the metropolis. He was tired. Tired of London, tired of the greasy pole, really tired of Hargreaves, tired of becoming someone he was never meant to be. Tired of hiding from the truth.

A ragged string of drookit parents, coaches, kids waiting as substitutes and assorted other onlookers, bordered one side of the pitch. Some of them huddled under umbrellas but, in truth, this kind of rain didn't have a single direction of flow, more cloud than shower head. An umbrella would be of limited use in terms of staying dry.

Running his eye along the line, Stark became aware that one of their number was staring rather intently back. A shiver of recognition danced along his vertebrae. Billy McDuff had grown up (and out, by the looks of him) but still possessed that dagger stare, still bore that swaggering demeanour of old. Stark tapped at the false tooth in his bottom jaw, remembering the pain and disorientation; lying on the floor as blood seeped from him, dark bruises forming, the McDuff brothers hobbling off nursing their own wounds.

For some unknown reason, he never really thought of what it might be like to confront ghosts like McDuff when he decided to come back home. Foolishness, naivety, denial? Who knew, but it was obvious the likes of McDuff would still be right where he left him all those years ago. Unlike Stark, Billy McDuff's parents couldn't have given less of a shit about him or his younger brother. Latchkey kids they used to be called. Neglected and abused would be the modern take on it. No encouragement to better; no support in adversity; no acknowledgement of success; no succour in distress. There were only three realistic options regarding the fate of the McDuff brothers during Stark's exile: prison, death by misadventure or nothing of any note whatsoever. Billy appeared to have chosen option three, but it would hardly be revelatory to discover option one also featured at some point in his history. Stark wondered if the same fate befell brother Malky. If Billy was the big, bad bruiser, Malky was the wee, nasty bastard. They made quite a pair right enough.

Firing up the ignition, Stark drove off. The restored power brought Everlong rolling out of the speakers; long since his favourite Foo's song, it never failed to hit the spot.

New colleagues were still to be encountered. The prospect didn't fill Stark with joy. Most Scottish folk are friendly by default. The majority would cause him no problems at all, welcome him even. However, there are always some who are all about routine, opinions set in concrete; change unsettles them. The 'other' is to be distrusted, tested, exposed and rejected.

Stark's stint with the MIT in London would be a big, unmissable bullseye for arrows of petty jealousy and disdain. There would be at least one new colleague (several if he was unlucky) with an overflowing quiver of ammunition. Big-headed; ideas above his station; trying to teach his granny to suck eggs; who did he think he was; too good for the likes of us I suppose; slumming it. For others, this return would be seen as weakness, ripe for exploitation: couldnae hack it; wonder what the real reason for him coming back here is; how come we're getting lumbered with the Met's cast-offs. Some would line up right in front of him but many would take aim from the rear, out of sight. Insidious undermining. Deep breaths, head down, do a good job, ignore it. That was the only way.

He drove up Broad Street, along Mar Street, to the roundabout where the police station and the Town Hall sat: a juxtaposition of the old and the new. The Town Hall an imposing nineteenth century fixture, the cop-shop a relatively modern, anonymous looking, brick-built affair. When he was a lad this space was occupied by a café and the bus station.

The Mar Café, scene of many an idle hour eating deep fried cuisine and playing video arcade games in the back room. Many of these games were making a revival in homes across the land as nostalgia-filled Dads and Granddads relived their misspent youth. In those days they were large pieces of furniture, over six feet tall and far from portable. It was weird in the extreme to think that things he used to consider cutting edge, cool and associated so strongly with his adolescence, now mostly existed in the memory of folks whose kids were old enough to bear their own progeny. Stark made a mental note to check out some online retailers and see if they stocked anything for his Playstation that would transport him back to those heady days of yore.

However, he wouldn't be darkening the door of his new employ today. The imagined aroma of roasting chicken and all the trimmings drew him past these landmarks towards home. Lunch with his Ma. Braw.

4. THE LONGEST NIGHT

Stella McDuff found herself trembling involuntarily. Earlier that evening she'd sworn her sister to secrecy, whatever that might mean in reality. Maureen's track record in the keeping a secret department suggested immediate disclosure to anyone within earshot, reachable by text or willing to take a phone call. With that in mind, she locked all the doors, closed the curtains, and turned out the lights. Squatting in the corner of the bedroom, her grip on the handle of the chef's knife fearsome.

Eventually, the ticket took up temporary lodgings in her bra. The last in a series of locations considered safe and easy to remember. Under the mattress, in the oven, in her shoe, under the kettle, all rejected. Inside the CD case of the Bee Gees Greatest Hits (on account of the song You Win Again) was her favourite unlikely place a robber might look, until even that lost out to the certainty of it being about her person at all times. Paranoia surged through her intermittently, causing her to shove her hand inside the undergarment to check the ticket was still there. It always was.

Billy refused to pick up her calls; his usual tactic when out on the lash without seeking permission or giving notice. Whether she'd be safer with him in the house was actually a moot point. They'd been married twenty years but Stella would be hard pushed to say she trusted Billy. Violent, moody, unreliable. The best she could muster in

11

the circumstances. Old circumstances without choices or escape routes. Pregnant at fifteen, Stella couldn't be sure it was Billy's but never admitted that to him. Catholic guilt and misguided romanticism about becoming a mother ensured the avoidance of an abortion, and Billy's uncharacteristic chivalry was grasped with grateful relief. If only she'd known.

William, about to turn twenty-one, still the apple of her eye, exiled in London, far away from the disapproval of his father and the bigots who taunted him throughout his teens. Oh, she missed him so much. Cameron, or Cammy as he was known, now approaching his sixteenth birthday, inherited or imitated all of his father's least desirable qualities. Jack, aged nine, heading toward being worse than sibling or father.

Her youngest rolled in just after ten o'clock unrepentant, uncommunicative, straight into his bedroom. There were more and more times recently when deep regrets about allowing her further impregnation by Billy McDuff rushed to the front of her mind.

Stella had been surrounded by ungrateful, casually violent, surly men all her life. Her father, a drunken yob who spent most of his adult life in prison before dying there from a heroin overdose. Uncle Gary, a drunken yob with an illegal fondness for his nieces that no policeman ever got to hear about. Her first proper boyfriend Derek, who liked to keep her in her place with the odd slap. Now, her husband and two of his sons. The only one who ever treated her right, William, far away, being himself.

The escape pod was primed with cash, ready to carry her away. But how? How would she escape from this triumvirate of relative reprobates? What choice did she have but to stay and share the winnings? Rich beyond her wildest dreams, but poorer than anyone could ever imagine.

The ticket said she needed to call a hotline, which she duly did. A very nice, calm young man took her details, told her they'd send someone out the next day. The call took no more than a few minutes but when they asked about one of their counsellors calling back, she panicked, said no. She would speak to them tomorrow.

A pack of cigarettes had gone by the wayside already, the emergency stash dipped into; the power station chimney at Longannet chuffed less ash into the atmosphere. But, even industrial levels of nicotine couldn't soothe her nerves. Sounds appeared amplified far beyond their normal levels. Every creak of the window frames, every toot of a car horn or raised voice in the street sent waves of fear and trepidation through her. Knuckles whitened as she clutched ever tighter on the knife handle.

The thumping on the door gave her such a start that Stella almost stabbed herself in the face. Holding her breath almost as tightly as the blade, she waited for the interloper to leave.

"Stella?"

The shout slurred out of Billy as he thumped the door again.

She sat still. Jack slept soundly, oblivious.

"Stella? Why the fuck's the door locked? Let me in you daft cow! I've no' got a key with me."

Ah, ever the gentleman. He forgets to take his key with him and that makes her a daft cow. A loaded, minted, millionaire of a daft cow as it happened.

The forcefulness of the thumping increased. Stella realised his next course of action would likely be to break a window or door frame. She could do without the hassle or unwanted attention that might bring with it, nor did she fancy the violent retribution he would mete out when he found her inside after all. Without enthusiasm, she went downstairs and let him in.

"What the fuck's going on, Stella? Are you fuckin deaf or something?"

Shoving past her, he headed for the kitchen, no doubt

seeking to gratuitously top up his blood alcohol levels. Stella didn't need a breathalyser to know he was well over the limit – legal or otherwise.

"I was in bed and I'm going back there the now. I'm really tired."

Billy barely registered this, staggering from the kitchen, can of beer in hand, toward the living room and his beloved television. So drunk he failed to notice she was fully clothed and holding a knife. So determined to avoid being contacted neither Stella nor Maureen were able to break the news that he was married to a millionaire.

Stella lit another cigarette and walked slowly up the stairs, her nerves no longer jangling. She patted her breast. Escape might be a possibility.

5. MORNING ALL

The alarm pushed its way into his sleeping mind like a queue jumper in a post office. Uncalled for, rude and picking on old folk barely able to defend themselves. Stark let out a long, low, mumbled, string of expletives. Lifting his phone and sliding the unlock bar across to cancel the ill-mannered shrieking, he rolled onto his back. Eyes glued shut, body worryingly relaxed, deep sleep and unforgivable lateness a distinct possibility. This was a big day. A first day...of sorts. No excuse for providing easy ammunition for any of the doubters. Although, none of the reasons for agreeing to start on a Sunday seemed good enough at this precise moment. With both eyes still heavily shuttered, he sat up, yawning and stretching, before finally allowing his lids to raise a fraction and reveal his surroundings.

It took a moment to get his bearings. His mother had long since moved from the house of his childhood, taking up residence in a very nice, modern, detached bungalow on the outskirts of the town. Quiet, well-to-do neighbours, with pensions and good jobs to fund their love of gardening, caravans and mountain biking.

Stark was in the guest room – a bland, inoffensive mix of floral and beige entirely in keeping with his mother's taste. A couple of small cabinets and a set of mirrored wardrobes kept the bed company. Parking elbows on knees and face in hands, he pushed his lips into a pout. The fact was, he couldn't be arsed.

After a few minutes of vegetating, drifting in and out of sentient thought, Stark forced limbs into motion and headed for the shower, remembering at the last minute whose house he was in. A pair of boxers were hauled on to spare his mother's blushes if she bumped into him in the hallway. Actually, it would be his blushes, his mother likely to exclaim something along the lines of 'Nothing I've not seen a thousand times before!'

The streaming flow of warm water finally brought him out of his stupor. Once dressed, he wandered into the kitchen to grab a bite of breakfast.

Mary Stark stood at the cooker, the glorious aroma of frying bacon, warming toast and fresh coffee floating toward her son as he sat down at the small, round table behind her. Tiny in stature but gigantic in heart and determination, life kept trying to knock the proverbial out of Mary. A beautiful, talented daughter driven to suicide by a drunken beast of a boyfriend; less than a year before, a loyal, loving husband sneaked up on by a heart attack that gave him no second chance; now the spectre of cancer and debilitating treatment. Each time, she dusted herself down and got on with it. Not a hard, emotionless denial but an optimistic stoicism. A determination to believe that everything would be ok, an innate gift for seeking the positive in life and grabbing hold of it. She was an inspiration to all who knew her.

"Morning, Ma. Ooh, something smells brilliant!"

"Morning, son, how're you doing? Looking forward to getting down the station and getting stuck in?"

"Aye, suppose so. It's a bit odd though, like a first day at a new school. No' sure how the guys here are going to take to a big shot from London coming into their team."

Mary turned to look at him, frowning. "Come on Adam, that's just daft. You're from round here. A local laddie, no' some posh English numpty wi' a degree and no idea what they're doing."

"Aye, but you know how some folk round here can be."

His mother shook her head ruefully, plated up his bacon and eggs, poured his coffee, buttered his toast and plonked all of it down in front of him with a satisfied smile on her face.

Stark grinned back up at her. "Thanks Ma, that looks magic!"

She returned the smile, poured her own coffee and took the chair across from him, sighing as she sat. The first light of the day began to creep across the sky outside, bird song in accompaniment. Stark thought he saw a weariness, a hint of fatigue she never usually demonstrated in the morning. Then again, he'd not stayed over for quite a while and, like it or not, the truth was his Ma was getting on a bit. He decided not to make anything of it.

"I saw Billy McDuff yesterday. Down at the Rugby Club. Has he got a laddie that plays fitba?"

Mary sipped her coffee and looked away into the distance. "Aye, probably. I think he's got three laddies; pretty sure the oldest left home, the middle one's about fifteen and the youngest maybe nine or ten."

"Must have been the youngest one. Funny seeing him again after all that time. He gave me the right evil eye by the way!"

Stark chuckled.

"No wonder, he wore that shiner for about a week!"

They both laughed at this.

"Whatever happened to wee Malky?"

"Ah, Malky McDuff. What a horrible, wee shite of a laddie that was! No' all his fault mind you. His parents were worse than useless. I think he did some time for assault but he's back living down in the Policies again. He was married to that Mo Watson. Do you mind her?" He nodded. He certainly did remember her, and her sister Stella – the root of his fateful altercation with the brothers McDuff. "But I'm no' sure if they're still together. They had a lassie called Tina who must be a teenager by now.

"Anyway, never mind that pair of wastrels, have you been in touch wi' Mickey or Tommo since you got back?"

Stark felt his face flush. Two of his oldest mates and they probably didn't even know he'd returned with some degree of permanency. Well, they certainly hadn't heard it from him.

"Em, naw, I never got around to it, Ma. Tommo's always away on the rigs whenever I try and phone him and Mickey, well, you know what he's like, Scarlet bloody Pimpernel!"

Mary shook her head. Her son was many things but good at keeping in touch with friends and loved ones was not high on his list of strong points. Still, she found it hard to get annoyed with him, bursting with love and relief at having him back under her roof – no matter how temporary the situation may prove to be. She would find a time to tell him about the cancer but it was not now. He had enough to worry about.

***

Stella tossed and turned all night, trying to relax enough to allow sleep to overcome her. It never did.

Billy stumbled upstairs about three o'clock and crashed out instantly, his nuclear-powered snoring not exactly helping her cause. The upside of his stupefying inebriation being it prevented any horrible groping, pleas for oral gratification or forced intercourse; any of which she might expect to be subjected to with a less emphatic intake of alcohol.

Cammy never appeared. No doubt lying in a gutter, in some girl's bed or on a stranger's floor. She'd long since given up trying to control or reason with her middle son. A lost cause, destined for jail or an early grave; she wished that made her sadder than it did.

At nine o'clock the alarm went off to rouse Billy and

send him on his way to the second football match of Jack's weekend. Like a lot of poor families, they secretly hoped sport, and football in particular, might offer their children an escape route from their situation. William was never sporty, which provided another excuse (as if another was needed) for his father to castigate him. Cammy rarely demonstrated prowess or interest in any sport other than boxing – unregulated, without gloves or ring, and usually involving the police as referees. Jack showed some promise as a centre forward for his school and his local junior side. The likelihood of him avoiding the pitfalls of drink, tobacco, drugs, poor diet, and de-motivation or distraction at the hands of jealous, less able contemporaries was slight. Nevertheless, for now, Jack played and Billy watched. The dutiful father and his dubious son would be gone for a couple of hours at least. Billy often indulged in a hair of the dog - the local boozer conveniently opened soon after the games finished - leaving the boy to his own devices. Even if he didn't do this, she should still have enough time to tidy up the house and meet the representative from the Lottery before they got back. The lad told her someone would be there at ten.

She'd turned off her phone, unplugged the landline and surreptitiously switched off Billy's phone as well. The last thing she needed was Maureen calling and giving the game away. Luckily, the silly madam spent the evening celebrating her new found status as sister of a millionaire, drinking herself into oblivion, and sleeping in until well gone midday.

Billy, hungover and grumbling, Jack tired and irascible from his late night, trundled off at about nine forty five. Stella tidied away the beer cans and ashtrays, washed up the dishes strewn throughout the lower floor, fished out a couple of cups and saucers from what was left of her good wedding china, and put on the kettle. At ten o'clock the doorbell rang and things were set in motion that could not be undone.

***

"Now then Adam, good to have you on board. I hope you're going to live up to your reputation and be a real asset to us here in Alloa. It might not be as gangsta as London but it has its own challenges all the same!"

DCI Don McLaren was an affable enough guy but, to use a good Scottish expression, he was also a bit of a dobber: slightly cringe-worthy in both appearance and turn of phrase. Late forties, but clearly stuck in the 1980's fashion-wise. Most baffling of all, the sunglasses perched on his head. It was early April in Scotland – he'd not be needing those anytime soon. Turned out he was known as Crockett around the station, in honour of Don Johnson's character in the TV series Miami Vice. There had also been a toe-curling attempt to ape a rapper's hand gestures when he referred to London as gangsta. Ah well, could be worse. At least he was friendly and avoided the confrontational bullshit that so permeated Hargreaves' every interaction with him.

"Thanks sir, I'm looking forward to it. Not much I'll miss about London to be honest – certainly not the gangsters."

"Aye, had a chance to join the Met myself a few years ago but the missus wouldn't leave her Ma and Da. Probably for the best, I've done ok for myself up here in the sticks."

Maybe just the first hint of resentment and a nose out of joint.

"Well, it's home for me, sir. Feels good to be back."

It surprised Stark how disingenuous this sounded as he said it: as if trying to justify himself, defend himself against subtle inference or implied criticism. A reflexive attempt at appeasement rather than a genuine expression of his feelings. He regretted it instantly.

"Right, aye, that's good. Anyway, I've decided to let you settle in easy today. Nothing pressing to attend to at the moment case-wise. I'll introduce you to a few of the guys and gals and you can get your desk and computer organised."

"Ok sir, that sounds fine. Happy to get stuck in if needed though."

"Naw, naw. Let's go out and meet the team."

They were a decent bunch. As predicted, a couple of them were frosty, one was outright hostile and the rest were welcoming and accommodating. His new team consisted of a DS Rourke, currently off on long-term sick, and a young DC called Ian Barr, not long qualified after a stint as a trainee. A bubbly, infectious enthusiasm permeated his speech and actions; no doubt too raw and inexperienced to have had such optimism ground out of him. Stark took it as a good sign, remembering the ebullience of his own early career, the man he used to be, working with Whistler Smith and putting the world to rights. Before London. He would enjoy working with Barr, he was sure of it.

An unremarkable morning passed with computer stuff, light banter, a few cups of tea, some dirty looks, orientation and other trivial tasks regarded as part of getting up to speed. It was all very well, but after a couple of hours, the novelty wore off.

"Where are you taking me for lunch then, Barr?"

"You asking me out, sir?"

The young cop grinned cheekily.

"Naw, but I might knock you out if you keep that pish patter up!"

"No' a lot of choice here, sir, eh."

"What, of patter, or restaurants?"

Barr grinned again.

In the days of his youth, Stark remembered the sentences of locals being peppered with the word 'ken'. The standard English equivalent being y'know. Usually delivered with a questioning intonation at the end of a sentence but also liberally sprinkled throughout, almost as a form of punctuation. Stark dropped ken into his sentences as enthusiastically as any other raised in the 'Wee County' of Clackmannanshire during the eighties and nineties. However, when he went to work in Glasgow, this phrase was the source of much hilarity or bemusement amongst folks who never used it. "Who's Ken?" being the most common response; genuine puzzlement or jibe the likely stimulus. Gradually, and without conscious forethought, it dropped from his vocabulary and the stint in England reinforced this banishment. Now, it seemed, ken had been usurped by 'eh' pronounced as ay. Still punctuating and implying a question, seeking agreement and confirmation of understanding, but somehow less characterful and definitely more irritating.

"Well, a sandwich will do for a start. We can manage that can we not?"

"Aye, a sandwich is doable right enough, sir."

They swung on jackets and headed for the exit. On the way, Stark stuck his head around the door of the DCI's office to ask if he wanted anything, but the boss wasn't there. McLaren must have left without saying anything. Could be indisposed in a lavatorial sense of course, but something about the room suggested a more permanent vacancy. Perhaps another hint at things to come, a certain lack of interest in his well-being, a tinge of unfriendliness even.

Much had changed around Alloa over the years he'd been gone. Some things for the better, others less so as far as Stark could tell. The town centre resembled so many around the UK these days. The High Street used to be a bustling collection of small shops and large chains. He remembered many hours spent hanging around a great wee shop called Europa Music, talking nonsense, thumbing through acres of vinyl albums, coveting countless of them but having so little money to acquire any. Turned out, Europa relocated to Stirling and, despite the onslaught from corporate chains and internet behemoths like Amazon, it was still trading. Still run by the same guy too – Ewen. A lot of small independent traders had departed and even the old Co-op department store seemed to have bitten the dust. However, Stark was encouraged by Barr's assertion that the Council were intent on regenerating the place, upgrading facilities and encouraging small businesses to return. There were signs of this happening with a wee shop selling fancy glass jewellery and the promise of a new restaurant or two on the way.

More important employers than the shops were no more; the once famous brewing industry and textile mills had closed their doors for ever, discharging their workforces into the arms of supermarkets and the social security system. It wasn't a ghost town but it was a lot quieter than the town centre of his childhood memories.

More positively, the railway was back. The line closed in 1968 and re-opened in 2008, giving the town a vital connection to Stirling and beyond, helping to attract those looking to work in Edinburgh or Glasgow but avoid paying the property prices of either city. A fair amount of new housing sprung up as a result and the population increased. Not all the big employers were gone either – the Glassworks remained, an industrial fixture from his youth that still dominated the skyline down by the River Forth.

As a town, Alloa covered all the bases – working class deprivation, to neatly tended middle class, to posh seclusion. The centre may have been quiet in a mercantile sense but he got the feeling of a town on the up, recovering from the trauma inflicted by Thatcher and her ilk. A long way to go, but hope a stronger part of its atmosphere than defeat.

Stark and Barr were heading back to the station after eating their sandwich when Stark had a revelation.

"Barr, I take it Orlandi's is still there?"

"Aye, of course, sir. You wanting an ice cream like?"

Stark found his mouth watering at the recollection of the ice cream of his youth.

"Do you know what Barr, I think I do. Is it still as good as I remember it?"

"Aye, it's good but it's no' that warm is it? An ice cream?"

"Do you know what, aye, fuck it. Let's go an' get a cone."

Barr was dubious but went along with his new boss.

The shop hadn't changed; location or interior décor as far as Stark could tell. He ordered a double scoop of vanilla on a cone and wasn't disappointed. It was too cold to be eating ice cream, it belted him right between the eyes, but he couldn't have given a smaller amount of faecal material. This glorious, frozen confection took him sailing back in time.

"Oh, man. Just as good as I remembered."

The rest of Stark's afternoon played out rather uneventfully and, as first days went, it could have been worse.

***

The sudden chiming of the doorbell caused Stella to jump. She smoothed down her T-shirt, stubbed out her cigarette and pulled back her greasy mop, holding it in place with an elastic band. She looked in the mirror near the front door – the woman reflected there was a disappointment, a failure, unconcerned with her appearance. That woman would be on her way very shortly.

"Hello, Mrs McDuff?"

A slim, well-dressed, middle-aged woman, carrying a leather folder stood outside on the step.

"Aye, you the woman from the lottery then?"

"That's right, Mrs McDuff. I'm Angela Curtis, pleased to meet you." Her arm snaked lithely from her side as she offered her hand to be shaken.

"Come in."

Billy sat at the bar, the dregs of his pint swirling in the bottom of the glass. Tipping it up, the last of the liquid slid down his gullet and he stood.

"Right Jonny, that's me away. Going home to get some grub, eh."

The barman nodded, lifting the empty glass from the counter top to dunk it in the sink of soapy water near the beer taps.

"Alright, catch you later, mate."

McDuff stepped into the street and sparked up a cigarette. The walk home would not take too long. He took out his mobile, noticing it was turned off. He didn't remember doing that but, as he was in the pub, when he should really be looking after his son, it was probably for the best. Switching it on, waiting for the usual compendium of Stella's tirades (both voicemail and text) to spring forth, he was pleasantly surprised to find no such accumulation had taken place. Shrugging, he dropped the phone back into his pocket.

As Billy reached home, the puzzling sight of Jack, sitting on the front step, greeted him. It wasn't a cold day, but there was no obvious reason the boy would choose to sit outside in his football kit, rather than go inside and get changed into something more appropriate.

"What are you doing sitting there?"

"There's nobody in, eh."

Billy frowned and fished out his key.

The house was quiet and abnormally tidy.

"Stella?"

No reply as the boy pushed past him and ran upstairs.

6. FRIENDS AND NEIGHBOURS

Graham Connelly pulled open the curtains a fraction and looked down through the crack the hurled brick created a week previous. Wire mesh spanned the frame, newly installed, for his protection; like viewing the world through the compound eyes of an insect. As usual, a monolithic mound of excrement adorned his garden path; wisps of steam curling upwards as the sun began to warm the air. Probably human, but potentially expelled from assorted mammalian digestive tracts. The contents of a wheelie bin decorated his front lawn, various items of household waste wafting lazily in the breeze. He couldn't see any obvious additions to the graffiti, but subtle augmentation was still a possibility.

The parole officer, social worker and clinical psychologist all assured him things should calm down. A backlash was inevitable once the news broke, he just had to ride out the storm. Eventually, someone else would become the focus of local ire, and he could return to anonymity and a buried past. In the meantime, they'd keep an eye on him and look for alternative accommodation. Well, that was six months ago. Things were going from bad to fucking unbearable.

From Friday to Sunday, he never left the house – only a medical emergency would convince him to break cover during this period. From Monday to Thursday, when the threat of drunken clubbers returning home in the early hours subsided, he would rise at four in the morning and visit the nearby hyper market, which traded round the clock. There were many American cultural imports he found irksome, but the provision of twenty four hour shopping proved invaluable to him. Of course, even at four o'clock in the morning it was necessary for him to wear a rudimentary disguise. Particularly since the publication of his picture in the local paper.

Graham Connelly spent six years in prison. He deserved it. In fact, he deserved a much longer sentence but got lucky: a couple of legal technicalities and a judge with a distorted world view. In the minds of most, the harassment and restrictions on his everyday life were merited; impositions to be tolerated, endured. Some might even say he should be grateful: the parents of his two young victims spent every waking hour engulfed in anguish he would never come close to experiencing. He didn't feel grateful though. Especially not when it came to those insufferable, relentless bastards the McDuffs. Their wrath never seemed to dampen or diminish, they always seemed to find the time to let him know what they would do to him if they ever got their hands on him, always seemingly able to squeeze at least one dose of verbal abuse or damage to his property into every day.

Peeking through the gap in his curtains, he noticed the youngest of his tormentors, Jack, sitting on the front step of his house in a football kit. It was so tempting to go down there and teach the little shit some manners, put him in his place. Show him a dark side neither of them would ever forget. Never going to happen though. The risk of either of the McDuff seniors appearing, as if by magic, was too great. Connelly may have been brave as a lion when it came to little kids, but he was more timid than a mouse with self-confidence issues when it came to facing those monsters. Right on cue, the boy's father rounded the corner, shooting a grievous glance towards Connelly's hiding place. He recoiled as if shot, allowing the curtains to close as he did so. Laying down on the bed, he switched on the television using a remote control, and settled in for another long day of boredom edged with anxiety. It wasn't all that different to prison really.

***

Mo Watson rolled over in bed and groaned. Her head felt heavy as a curling stone; blood pounding through her temples like fists hammered on tables; veins and arteries shrieking in protest at the lack of hydration; every receptor cell in her brain crying out in unison for nicotine to come and offer its sweet salve. Her hand flapped about on the bedside cabinet like a recently landed fish, clamping down on the packet with relief. She transferred the one remaining white stick of death and restoration to her mouth in a motion driven more by reflex than conscious thought. The lighter and its life-giving flame completed her mission and, as the noxious fumes and poisonous chemicals filled her lungs, Mo began to feel a bit better.

Sitting up resumed the torture with a vengeance. Quivering, the fists in her temples became jack hammers, her stomach lurched, a prickling hot flush, then a shuddering cold sweat swept over her skin. She rushed for the bathroom, only just making it in time to eject the previous night's kebab and a substantial quantity of white wine into the toilet bowl. Mo knelt there, gripping the porcelain, waiting for a reprise. After a couple of minutes, it became apparent her body was satisfied it had rid itself of all its unwelcome gastric guests and she felt able to stand.

Filling a glass from the tap, she sloshed a mouthful of water around, removing the foul remnants of vomit. She spat it out, rinsed it away; the next sip taken gingerly, aware that her stomach might be far less welcoming of the fluid than her throbbing cranium. A few more minutes gathering herself followed. A cursory set of ablutions and she trudged downstairs to the kitchen to put on the kettle.

Hot, black coffee made, Mo plodded through to the living room. Jesus, it was a bloody pigsty! Discarded takeaway cartons and wrappers, bottles, glasses - some still holding residuary substances, most empty. An overflowing ashtray, or two, a tatty Argos catalogue, a broken-heeled shoe, her crumpled jacket. Streamers from party poppers and sticky lines of that annoying silly-string that people found it hilarious to squirt on one another when they were drunk. Bloody stuff was an absolute bitch to get off the upholstery – especially if allowed to congeal overnight. The fug in her head was preventing her piecing together the events precipitating what, even by her standards, was an epic piss-up.

Mo shuffled over to the foot of the stairs, which terminated near the front door, and shouted upwards.

"Tina?"

No answer from her wayward offspring. Probably still sleeping off her own hangover. Of course, the lassie was under age, but they all did it. At least Mo was keeping an eye on her daughter, making sure she stayed safe. Better than being a hypocrite or in denial. Her parents never had a clue she was getting bladdered on a regular basis from the age of twelve. Right enough, her Dad was usually too out of his face on smack or banged up in prison to notice she was breathing, never mind drinking, but still.

"Tina? You awake, hen?"

Nothing.

She took a few minutes to locate her mobile phone; under a kebab wrapper, on the floor, near the couch. The display told her it was 13.45. She seemed to recall noticing it was around five thirty when she'd crashed upstairs to bed.

Her head was clearing, perhaps the coffee was doing its job. Maybe it was her fifth cigarette since she woke or the little pull on the half-empty bottle of gin. Hair of the dog. A tried and tested, entirely legitimate cure for a hangover.

Lottery, Stella, holy shit! Her sister was a millionaire, ergo Mo was rich!

She checked her phone for missed calls. There was only one – from Billy. That was odd, why hadn't Stella been trying to get her? She said she was meeting the woman from the lottery that morning. Mo insisted she should be there to make sure all went well. However, the drinking and revelry caused her to sleep in and Stella hadn't bothered to stir Mo from her alcoholic slumber.

The short, sharp message from Billy was delivered with his usual charm and panache.

"Mo, where the fuck is Stella? She wi' you? Tell her I want my fuckin dinner, and if she thinks I'm looking after the bairns while she gets pished wi' you, you fuckin lush, she's got another thing coming."

A lush? Who the fuck did he think he was talking to? Still, despite the undeniable fact that Billy was a cheeky bastard and a complete arsehole, this wasn't right. Where was Stella? She'd just won a total bloody fortune on the lottery, then gone AWOL. He clearly didn't have a clue about the familial windfall or he'd have mentioned it.

The door nearly shook loose from its frame under the assault Billy launched on it. Mo dropped her coffee mug in fright, the residual cold liquid in the bottom of it creating another dark smudge on her already copiously stained carpet. She grabbed for the handle and yanked the door open.

"What the fuck's your problem, Billy, eh? Ring the bell like any normal person would you!"

Billy's face conveyed his extreme displeasure at both having to come in search of his wayward spouse and at being abused by her inebriated sister.

"Ach, away you go you drunken cow. Where is she?"

"Do you mean Stella?"

"Don't get wide wi' me Mo, or I'll gladly punch your fuckin lights out. Where is she?"

"What a fuckin charmer you are, Billy McDuff, eh.

Threatening women make you feel tough does it? I never understood what my sister saw in you."

"Look, I'll no' ask you again. Where the fuck is Stella?"

He moved toward her, fists balled, a black cloud of fury hanging over him. Even with Dutch courage Mo knew not to push him any further. He would be true to his word, she knew that to her cost. Instinctively, she stepped back using the door to shield herself.

"She's no' here, right. I'm just out my bed after a heavy night and I've no idea where she is."

"Really? You lying cow!"

Billy barged in, sending her sprawling backwards onto the staircase, jarring her tail-bone on one of the steps. He ignored her howl of pain and set about checking every room in the house for Stella.

Back in the living room empty-handed, he pointed a fat, accusing finger at Mo.

"Right, so she's no' here the now, but I know she's up to something, and I know you're in on it – you always are. You need to get round to our house and look after Jack. I've got to go out."

Mo held the still-tender base of her spine and thought about clearly identifying the orifice into which he should insert that idea. However, it suited her to go round to Stella's. Her sister must have gone out to buy something nice with her new found fortune, enjoying herself before bugger lugs here got a hold of it and she was left with nothing. She knew the greedy bastard too well. Maybe Stella was, right now, buying Mo a fancy sports car or a designer hand bag. Of course, that was it. Stella. Good old Stella, always looking out for other folks.

Mo smiled knowingly and assumed her most sarcastic tone.

"Ok, as you asked so nicely, Billy. I'll go round once I've got dressed."

Billy stormed away without hint of gratitude or acknowledgement.

Mo climbed the stairs, wincing with each step, her coccyx stinging and throbbing. On the top landing, she knocked on Tina's bedroom door. Still no reply. She should be awake considering Billy crashed in uninvited a few moments previous. Actually, it now seemed odd there hadn't been howls of protest and the sudden appearance of a teenager impersonating a rattlesnake. Tina was too young and hormonal to fear her uncle. Mo pushed the door open and looked in. The unmade bed was devoid of daughter. She frowned and shrugged. Tina must have been less affected by her alcohol intake than Mo; up before her and gone out by the looks of things. Mo wasn't too concerned, she'd turn up when she got hungry.

Mo showered, her earlier attempts at cleaning, post-regurgitation, proving inadequate for a public appearance. She decided against using the dryer on her hair; it wasn't that cold out and it would take too long. Going for the casual, comfortable look, she flung on a tracksuit and trainers. At the foot of the stairs she took another swig of gin, just to settle her nerves and dull the pain in her back, locked the front door and set off.

The walk to Stella's house didn't take long. She used the back door, finding that interfering bitch from the Social Work sitting at the kitchen table, drinking Stella's tea, bold as brass.

"What the fuck are you doing here?"

"Hello Maureen, nice to see you too. I brought Cammy home after a bit of a run-in with the law. When I got here Stella and Billy weren't in and Jack was by himself, so I stopped in until an adult got here," Kirsty Barr replied breezily, ignoring the aggression and profanity aimed at her.

Mo looked at her with equal parts disdain and suspicion.

"Cammy's old enough to watch his brother though, eh. So why did you no' just do one?"

"Yes, well, technically, he's not really old enough, but in any case, he gave me the slip not long after we got back. I was keen to talk to his Mum or Dad about what happened, so I stayed."

It was hard to remain positive and not rise to the taunts but years of practice kicked in automatically.

"Right, well, I'm here now so you can get lost. I'll wait in with the wee man until his Ma or Da gets back."

Kirsty stood, rinsed out her cup in the sink and showed herself out, Mo's disapproving stare boring into her as she went.

***

"You been down the Bottom End the day again?" Ian Barr shouted above the noise of the boiling kettle toward the living room where his wife, slumped on the couch, still wearing her jacket and shoes, gawped at the muted television with de-focused eyes.

"Aye. It's been one of them days."

Kirsty Barr liked being a social worker, most of the time. After seven years, she'd learnt her trade well, progressing up the ranks to assume seniority in her office. Even challenging, harrowing cases could be rewarding and satisfying. The pelters her profession took, from the tabloid press in particular, would knock the confidence of anyone involved in such work, but Kirsty took pride in disregarding their brickbats and doing the best job she possibly could. Sometimes, the people who least wanted her help were the most grateful to have received it. However, even she was losing patience with the McDuffs.

Ian walked into the living room and placed the cup of tea on a coaster on the coffee table in front of her. She smiled in gratitude, reached for it and took a weary sip, cradling the cup in both hands afterwards, allowing the warmth to soothe her. He carried his own mug over to the armchair and sat down.

"Don't tell me. The McDuffs?"

She nodded and sipped again.

"You no' stopping then?" he said, winking at her.

"Oh, aye. I was away in a wee world there, eh."

Kirsty put down her cup and went out to the hallway, slipped off her shoes, pushed her feet into a pair of slippers instead, and hung up her coat.

Back on the couch, she curled her legs underneath herself and resumed her tea sipping.

"What have that bunch of no-hopers been up to now?"

"Oh, just the usual, eh. Their laddie Cammy, was out all night, got roaring drunk, crashed out on a park bench, then got caught having a pee in some old dear's garden this morning. She called your lot, who called me and I took him home to find his parents nowhere to be seen and his wee brother home alone...again. Sat about the house for a couple of hours, being stared at and ignored at the same time, then copped a load of abuse from the auntie who turned up and said she'd look after them until Billy got back. A perfect Sunday afternoon off – not!"

Ian shook his head.

"They're a shower of bampots the McDuffs. I don't know what you did to deserve being allocated them by your boss."

"She's no' got any choice, Ian. The other lassie in the office is too green, eh, and as for Sullivan, he's worse than useless, and terrified of Billy McDuff. That leaves yours truly holding the baby."

"Aye, it's a pity that baby is Damien from the fuckin Omen!"

"Hiy, language you! I get enough of that at work, I don't need it at home an' all, eh."

"Ok, fair enough."

She placed her now empty cup on the table and reached for the remote.

"What do you want to watch?"

"No' bothered really. Is the Omen on?"

She flung a cushion at him and they both laughed like drains. It was at times like these they forgot their troubles and realised why they fell in love with each other. Kirsty wished these moments would happen more often.

7. MISSING YOU

Stark and Barr stood outside the door of Mo Watson's house, waiting for her to answer. Stark felt uneasy, nervous. A strange return to his days as a rookie, maybe a return to further back than that. Day two in the new job certainly seemed to be promising something pretty different from the insouciance of day one.

Eventually, the lady of the house deigned to respond to their knocking. Mo Watson looked nothing like the person Stark expected to see standing in the threshold. To coin a phrase his father liked to use, she looked like she'd had a hard paper round. Dank, bleached-blonde hair drooped down limply from her head, framing a gaunt face with sunken eyes, poor complexion and lips so thin they were almost invisible. The yellowish hue of her skin indicated a drink problem, backed up by the way her casual sports clothes hung baggily from her narrow frame. She looked in dire need of a good feed; something containing more solid than liquid for a change.

A frown crossed her face, the cigarette she held went to her mouth and she folded her arms defensively across her chest. She may well have called the police but it didn't mean she needed to be happy about it.

"Aye?"

"Hello Maureen, this is Detective Constable Barr, and I'm Detective Inspector..."

"Adam Stark. Is that you right enough? Fuck's sake.

What are you doing here?"

"Em, you called us about your missing daughter, Maureen. So, here I am. Can we come in?"

Mo stepped aside and pulled the door slightly further ajar.

"Aye, alright. Come in then."

Once they were in, she looked back and forth nervously along the street, checking for anyone who might have spotted the coppers entering her house, before closing the door.

They entered straight into the living room: a small, dingy space, evidently it was a long time since its last redecoration. Everywhere they looked, signs of slowly accumulated neglect, with nothing to indicate Mo made any effort to tidy in anticipation of visitors arriving; this applied as much to her as it did to the house.

"Sit down."

This would have been a lot easier if there was an uncluttered spot to do so.

"Where should we do that, Maureen?" asked Barr.

She huffily lifted aside a couple of magazines and a crumpled t-shirt to make some space on the settee. It forced Barr and Stark to sit rather closer together than they might like but it shaded standing.

The former Mrs Malcolm McDuff paced anxiously back and forth in front of them, puffing away at her cigarette, failing to take a seat of her own. Although hardly a towering presence, she looked down upon the two cops from her elevated vantage point; it made Stark even less comfortable.

"Maureen, do you mind sitting down please? It's hard to concentrate with you walking up and down like that."

She pouted, sighed and sat on the arm of a chair.

"Alright then Maureen, tell us everything you can about Tina, and why you think she's gone missing."

Stark thought his voice sounded disconnected, ill at ease with being back among the spectres of his past.

"I don't think she's missing, she is missing okay! We had a party, no' last night but the night before, when we found out..." Just in time, she remembered her promise to Stella, she wouldn't break it for the sake of a couple of coppers, "...anyway, we had a party. She went off to bed late, I went up a bit later, eh. Next morning, she wasn't in her room when I checked but I didn't think anything of it."

"What time in the morning was that, Maureen?" asked Barr, jotting details in his notebook.

"Aye, well, it might have been more like afternoon. It was a late one. A few bevvies involved. Probably about two o'clock I think. Anyway, nothing to worry about at that point – I just thought she'd gone out to one of her friends or something. Then Billy came round and asked me to watch wee Jack for a bit, which I did, eh. But, when I got back there was still no sign of Tina."

"And, what time did you get back?"

"About ten o'clock."

"Have you tried phoning her and checking with her friends?"

"Aye, of course. I gave it until this morning, just in case she was at a pals, but she never came back in time for school. She's no' answering her mobile and none of her pals saw her yesterday. That's why I phoned you lot, eh. I just want you to find my wee lassie for me."

A shadow of vulnerability swept across her face, tears dropped down her cheeks. Sniffing, she wiped them away, stubbed out her cigarette and immediately lit another, hands shaking.

"Okay Maureen, we'll do our best to help you. How old is Tina?" asked Stark.

"Fifteen, sixteen next month."

"Is she Malky McDuff's bairn as well?"

"Aye, more's the fuckin pity!"

"She wouldn't have gone round to see him then?"

The look Mo sent Stark's way might have taken his

head off his shoulders if it had been any keener.

"That bastard's no' allowed anywhere near Tina after what he did."

Stark looked to Barr who grimaced, realising he should have given Stark a heads up on the familial politics of the McDuffs.

"What did he do, Maureen?"

"Locked the poor wee mite in a cupboard then went out to the pub, got totally pissed and left her there all night. Next day, when I get back from my Maw's I find her still there, sitting in a pool of her own pish, terrified and starving. He's lying in his bed, still fuckin comatose wi' drink. That was it for me, eh. I chucked him out and got the court to put a banning order on him. All he got for it apart from that was a community order and sent on a course about parenting. I mean, what the fuck kind of punishment is that? The man's a fuckin headcase, she's far too scared of him to ever go round there."

The trauma of relaying this outburst forced her hand on the alcohol front. Reaching for a half-empty, half litre of gin on the coffee table, Mo screwed the top off, and imbibed straight from the bottle.

"Right, sorry, I didn't realise. What about Billy or Stella? Have they no' heard from her either?"

Mo sniffed. "Naw, in fact, Stella seems to have gone AWOL as well."

The cops exchanged glances again.

"What do you mean, Maureen?"

"Billy says Stella went out sometime on Sunday morning and she's no' come back, eh."

"Do you think Stella and Tina might be together?"

A penny dropping, dots being joined.

"Em, aye, well, maybe. Naw. I don't know. Suppose they could be."

"Have you called Stella this morning?" asked Barr.

"Aye, but she's no' picking up. Phone goes straight to answer machine."

40

"Can we have a look in Tina's bedroom?"

Mo nodded, leading them upstairs to the girl's bedroom. Nothing unusual. A standard teenage girl's midden; floor and bed strewn with discarded clothes, CD's, make-up and magazines. The walls adorned with posters and cuttings of pop stars, minor celebrities and other cultural fluff.

"Have you touched anything since Saturday night?"

"Naw."

"Right, well, please leave it as it is. If we need to come back, it's best you don't move anything, just in case.

"Oh, by the way, was there anyone else round here for that party?"

"Naw, it wasn't really a proper party. Just a wee blow out. Spur of the moment, eh."

Stark knew Mo was holding something back, being evasive about the reason for throwing the party. He decided to let it ride for now. She was already defensive and traumatised, agitating her further wouldn't help him find the girl any quicker, it might actually slow things down. The drink didn't help either. He could always come back to it later.

"We'll go round and speak to Billy. Have you got anyone to keep you company?"

Mo looked at the floor, sweeping her foot back and forth slightly. "No' really, Stella would usually have been my rock in this sort of situation."

"Do you want us to send round a female liaison officer?"

"Naw, do I fuck! I don't need some nosy, interfering copper sitting about my house, drinking my tea, and pretending to give a shit about me and my family."

"Alright, that's your choice, just thought I'd offer."

"Am I supposed to be grateful or something? I remember you when you were getting your lamps punched out by Billy and Malky, eh. Thought you were something special back then and you obviously still do!

"Stop standing here wasting my time and get on wi' finding my wee lassie."

Door firmly shut behind them, Stark and Barr walked the few streets down towards Billy McDuff's. Back on his old stomping ground, Stark felt the warmth of childhood on his back.

The Bottom End had a reputation. Some of it earned, much of it myth. He remembered good people as well as bad. Characters like Billy and Malky counterbalanced by neighbours who'd be there in a second when you really needed them. Stark remembered fun, football, riding his bike, building gang huts, sexual awakening. Sure, there was poverty, violence, drugs. But, like anywhere, it couldn't be painted in clear black and white. Even Billy wasn't without redeeming features; if you looked really hard for them. The loss of so many local jobs hit the area hard, took a lot of hope away. Somehow, it still felt like home – even after all their time apart. Stark would always be a Bottom Ender but that didn't make him a junkie, a dole dodging scrounger or a Ned. There had always been more to the place than that. Still was.

"What was she on about in there, sir? You had run-ins wi' the McDuffs then have you?"

Stark thought about what to tell the youngster. Was he fishing for salacious gossip or just naturally curious following the remark made? Bare minimum.

"Aye, well, I used to live round here, mind. I know the McDuff lads from then. Billy was in my year at school, Malky's a couple of years younger. Always fighting, always in bother. Seems some things never change."

"Looking forward to seeing Billy again then, sir?"

"Oh, aye, can hardly contain my fuckin excitement."

8. VISITING TIME

Stark knocked on Billy McDuff's door and waited, stomach knotting, mouth desiccating, a fidget developing in his fingers. His one-time nemesis, now involved in a case he was working on, about to appear at any moment. He badly wanted to feel more assured, controlled: like a detective inspector with nearly twenty years policing under his belt.

The door opened.

"Fuckin hell. Adam Stark. So, it was you I saw hanging about the park the other day then?"

"Aye, it was me right enough, Billy."

Stark held up his warrant card.

"Thought you were down in London."

"Aye, I was, but I've moved back here now."

The blubbery, unkempt, tattooed figure occupying the doorway glared with as much ferocity as the more svelte, tidy, younger one ever did.

"So, what the fuck do you want?"

"We've just been round to Maureen's, she's worried about Tina. She went out yesterday morning and she's not come home. I wondered if maybe you'd heard from her?"

"Naw, I've no' seen Tina for a few days. She's likely just round at one of her pal's houses."

"Aye, maybe, but Maureen can't raise her on the phone and none of her pals has heard from her."

Frowning, McDuff folded his massive arms, resting

them on the small hillock that was his belly. "Look, the lassie's nearly fifteen and, let's face it, her Maw likes a bevvy. She probably got pissed off about something that drunken bitch did and went away for a couple of days. No big deal, eh. Now if that's it, I've got other things to be getting on wi'."

Stark didn't find Billy's attitude surprising. Lots of kids on the estate (including Billy McDuff in his formative years) needed to develop a sense of independence very early in life. It wasn't the done thing for their parents or other close family to show too much love, care or affection. It toughened them up, got them ready for the real world; it was the example set when they were kids. Stark decided to enquire about the other alleged absconder.

"Maureen says Stella's gone missing as well. Is that right?"

"It's none of that nosy cow's business and it's none of yours either!"

"I'm only asking coz I wondered, if Stella had gone off somewhere, do you think Tina might be with her?"

"Look, like I said, I've got no idea where Tina is. A storm in a bloody tea-cup if you ask me. As for Stella, then she's an adult and can do what the fuck she wants. So, are we done here?"

"Aye, that'll do for now. Let us know if you hear anything though, won't you?"

"Aye, right. Whatever."

With that, the door slammed in their faces.

Barr grinned at Stark.

"That went pretty well I thought, sir!"

"Piss off! Right, let's go and talk to Malky."

Barr grinned again.

"Don't even think about it," said Stark.

Billy hated being in the presence of any policeman but finding out that prick Stark was back in Alloa really riled him. He'd done well not to react with his fists. The incident all those years ago still crept about in the corners of his memory, a festering sore of humiliation and regret he thought might have healed. Stark's reappearance started the pus oozing again. If Billy got the chance, he'd put some things right and, this time, there'd be no walking away with his tail between his legs.

Stella was missing as it happened. She still hadn't come home and Billy was far from chuffed about it. Billy pottered about, achieving nothing of any consequence – a regular Monday morning for him - Jack and Cammy off to school. Well, he'd seen them leave the house at the requisite time, whether they actually made it through the front door of the school would be less certain. The Social seemed to think it was a big deal that his children missed so much schooling but he genuinely didn't care. School was a total waste of time. No jobs, no need for qualifications. There was an admirable resourcefulness required to escape capture as often as the boys did and stay just below the threshold which might trigger legal action against Billy or Stella. As far as Billy was concerned, this skill would be much more useful to them than any mathematical equation or poem.

***

Greg Marshall felt the tears come again, hating himself for the weakness, the self indulgence, but unable to fully control his emotions. It happened roughly once a day now, a gradual increase in frequency over the past few weeks. He gazed down at little Brandon, feeling as if every muscle fibre in his heart was about to stretch beyond its capacity and cause a massive explosion in his chest. Love, guilt, regret, fury, impotence. All these things surged through him in waves, sometimes simultaneously. This tiny little bundle of innocence, unaware of his surroundings, oblivious to the momentous impact he'd had on Greg's

45

life, so totally and utterly dependent on his father.

The doorbell snapped Greg from his trance. He gently kissed his son on the forehead, then went to answer.

"Hi, Kirsty, come in."

The smiling social worker did so, wiping her feet on the mat, responding to Greg's gesture by handing him her coat to be hung on a peg in the downstairs cloakroom.

"Cup of tea?"

"That would be nice thanks, Greg."

Kirsty Barr sometimes felt as if her back teeth were floating she drank so much tea every day. She'd gone through a phase of trying to politely decline but folks were so insistent. It's one of those tasks that people like to undertake to give themselves something to do. Sometimes a distraction from an awkward or difficult moment, perhaps the only gesture of gratitude they feel able to make or can afford. Whatever, she had long since given up protesting.

"Black, no sugar, right?"

"Yes, that's right, thanks."

Kirsty sat down on the couch in the living room. The removal of milk and sugar reduced both calorie intake and improved quality control. Some people's tea with milk and sugar in could be repellent.

The rumble and hiss of the boiling kettle drifted through from the kitchen. Clattering crockery and the gentle tinkle of stirring followed before Greg returned with tea and biscuits on a tray, which he placed on the table in front of Kirsty.

She smiled at him as he dropped wearily into the armchair opposite her.

"So, how are things today, Greg?"

"Oh, you know. Hard, emotional, upsetting, depressing and brilliant – the usual!"

He grimaced rather than grinned. This was a regular 'joke' they shared, delivered without irony or any real humour. All of those things were true every day for Greg.

Acidic, corrosive adversity in whacking great doses, neutralised intermittently by a smile, gurgle or fleeting reaction from Brandon.

"And, how's the wee man?"

"I refer the honourable lady to the answer I gave previously."

Again, the humour was flat, robotic. A lame attempt to divert a tiny fraction of his entire attention away from the hopelessness and suffocating sorrow that engulfed him.

"What's the latest state of play regarding the treatment? Any more news?"

Tears appeared to spring up in the man's eyes and Kirsty suddenly felt awful for having asked.

"There's no change. Still can't get them to agree to it on the NHS. The doctor says it's too expensive. The truth is, the money it would cost might save the lives of six or seven other wee kids. I get it, but it doesn't make it any easier to accept, eh."

"Yeah, it's a terrible thing having to decide who can and can't have stuff done based on money. I'm glad it's no' my job."

An awkward silence ensued. Both of them unsure how to respond next without going down a path leading toward argument, frustration and anger. Kirsty eventually broke ranks.

"Can I have a gander at the wee chap?"

"Aye, sure. He's in his cot."

They walked through an archway separating the living room from the dining area: no longer used for eating but instead serving as a playroom and bedroom for Brandon. Bright, stimulating colours abounded, a multitude of toys adorned the floor, and three different mobiles spiralled from the ceiling. The cot took centre-stage. She couldn't fault the guy. It was a nice house, well tended.

Kirsty gazed down at the tiny, stricken child and swallowed hard. This was the visit she found tougher than any other. The vice-like grip on her emotions, a skill honed over the years spent dealing with distressing cases, came perilously close to slipping free. Her own sorrow coursed through her veins like an icy spike. She looked away and let the welling in her eyes subside before facing Greg again.

"You're doing an amazing job, Greg. He's very lucky to have you."

Greg looked at his feet, embarrassed, flattered, sad.

"Well, I think I'll get on my way and leave you boys to it. Oh, by the way, did you hear about the McDuffs?" Kirsty again cut the tension with her breezy tone. It was important in her job to try and keep positive; for her own sake as much as the clients'.

"No, what have The Addams Family been up to now then?"

Greg fetched her coat and helped her on with it.

"Ha! Very good, I've no' heard that one before. Well, the rumour I've heard is, they've won the lottery!"

"Oh for fuck's sake! Sorry, excuse my French," he added, blushing at his uncharacteristic foul-mouthed outburst. "Is there no justice in the world? If ever you needed proof there was no God, then there it is, right there!"

"Well, you could have a point, Greg. Might no' be true of course, you know what this place is like for rumours, eh. Anyway, I need to get on. I'll see you same time next week. Cheerio the now."

"Aye, see you later. Thanks for dropping in, eh."

Greg watched Kirsty walk off up his path to her car. She was a really nice woman. Kind, considerate, empathetic...sexy. He shook his head. What was wrong with him? He closed the door and headed for the playroom, the plaintive mewing of his son drawing him back to the task in hand.

***

William McDuff sat in a café a few streets from King's

Cross station, scrolling through Facebook updates on his phone. The butterflies in his stomach increased when he noticed the time – just ten more minutes and she'd be here.

London saved William. He could be the man he always wanted to be, free from bigotry, violence, isolation and disapproval. Graduating from Art school, starting his own business, buying a flat, falling in love – all of these things happened in London. The only cloud hanging over these wonderful, life-affirming achievements was leaving Stella behind. Leave her to suffer at the hands of a brutish lout who neither loved nor respected her. Leave her to try and raise a couple of feral brats who probably loved her but rarely proved it. Leave her to have her massive heart gradually ground into dust.

Stella loved him unconditionally. Never judged, never taunted, never implored him to change. When he left, her heart broke, but she understood why he had to go. She didn't try to stand in his way, no emotional blackmail, no guilt trip. Visits home had been infrequent and painful thanks to his father and his execrable siblings, so when Stella called to say she was coming to London, he was thrilled. The first time she'd ventured there and, apparently, with big news to tell. Something intriguing, something she was saving until she got there.

William sipped the last of his coffee, dropped a tip into the saucer and walked out into the street. Five minutes to go. He hurried toward the station, determined to be in situ when her train came in.

***

Malky wore his contempt like a forcefield, deflecting any attempts at rapport or normal human interaction. He made Billy seem warm and welcoming in comparison.

"So, you've no idea where Tina could be then?" asked Stark.

49

"Naw, that's the third time I've told you that, eh. You got a fuckin hearing problem or something?"

"Malky, I'll tell you again, and for the last time, please don't use foul and abusive language towards me or I'll be forced to arrest you for a breach."

Malky fumed, grimacing, shaking his head so frequently it risked coming loose.

"Now, as I understand it, you're barred from contact with Tina. Is that right?"

"Aye."

"Due to an incident of abuse that took place a few years ago?"

"No comment."

"Well, Maureen, your ex-wife, told us you locked Tina in a cupboard and left her there overnight. Is that what happened, Malky?"

Stark was loving this, rushing back to those good old days, when he and Malky were teenage rivals. Difference now was, Stark held more cards. He was police, Malky couldn't react how he wanted and Stark could wind him up with impunity. The rage in Malky was either going to spill over into an arrestable offence or drive him to the point of cerebral haemorrhage. A win win.

"I'm no' answering any questions about all that shite. If you, or that scheming bitch, think I've got something to do wi' Tina going missing, you charge me an' take me down the nick. Otherwise, fuckin leave me alone an' get on wi' finding out where she is."

"Ok, you won't mind if we have a wee look around then?" asked Stark, waving his red rag for all it was worth.

"Naw, go ahead. It'll no' take you long, this isn't exactly a fuckin mansion."

Barr got up and went off to inspect the other rooms in the flat.

"You think I don't know what you're doing, Stark?" hissed Malky.

"What's that, Malky?"

50

"Trying to get your own back for all them years ago when me and Billy kicked fuck out of you. This is pure harassment. I could put in a complaint about you, eh."

"Don't flatter yourself, Malky. I'm just doing what I'm supposed to do when a wee lassie goes missing an' it turns out her Dad has a conviction for abusing her. You're lucky we haven't arrested you."

Malky's piss boiled in his bladder, nothing he could do.

"All clear, sir," said Barr as he returned to the living room.

"Ok, well, that'll do us for now, Malky. If we need you, we know where to find you and if you hear anything from Tina, be sure to let us know. Here's my card."

Malky refused to take it, standing up, arms folded, a reddening fury in his skin. Stark laid it on the arm of the chair and stood up himself.

"We'll see ourselves out," said Stark.

"Fuckin right you will, you prick!" muttered Malky as they left.

Back out on the street, Stark and Barr stopped at the kerb. Stark checked his mobile and pager for messages or texts.

"Wee Malky's no' that keen on you, sir, is he?"

"I don't know what you could possibly mean, Barr."

Stark smirked. It felt so good to get stuck into that bastard McDuff again. So many times when they were young, hiding behind his brother's substantial back-up, the little turd would taunt Stark. Well, that was never going to happen again.

"Aye, an' you were loving giving him pelters as well, eh."

"No, not at all, Ian. Just doing my job."

They both laughed and got back in the car.

"Can't say I blame you taking that attitude wi' him, sir. He seems like a nasty piece of work."

"Aye, he certainly is, Barr. Always has been."

9. ENEMIES IN A STATE

"Aye, it's they Polish bastards that are to blame, eh. Taking all the jobs from us local folk. No' just that though, they get all the council houses an' all. Straight to the top of the list while folk like me get hee haw. There's fuckin thousands of them in the toon these days. Fuck's sake, one of them even coaches the bloody fitba for the laddies. It's a fuckin liberty man!"

Malky McDuff's sermon on modern Scottish life came straight from the distorted, one-eyed headlines and misinformed pages of his two favourite newspapers. Billy only half-listened, he'd heard it all before. This preaching and whining normally started the moment Malky parked his backside on a bar stool, drink in hand; a pretty regular occurrence in itself. It turned out, the root of all of Malky's woes could be traced back to external sources. The lack of a job, the stretch behind bars, Maureen leaving him, the crappy flat, the lack of disposable income. The gospel according to Malky proclaimed none of these misfortunes befell him directly as a consequence of his own actions - the blame needed to be laid at the door of a series of others.

Billy let him rant. He agreed with some of it but the bits he disagreed with were not worth the hassle debating. Debating, that was a laugh. Malky didn't do debating. He did telling you, shouting you down and, if that still failed to convince you he was right, beating you. The latter point was not something Billy need concern himself with, but the ranting and shouting got on his nerves. No compromise, no concession, no humility. Billy got it, he understood the root of it, he just couldn't be arsed with it.

"Did that wanker Adam Stark visit you yesterday as well?" asked Malky, suddenly changing tack.

"Aye, fuckin Detective Inspector now, back from London but still just a big prick wi' a big opinion of himself, eh."

"Aye, arrogant bastard. Had the fuckin cheek to imply that I'd got something to do wi' Tina going missing."

Wonder why he might have thought that, thought Billy.

"What's going on by the way? Has Tina showed up yet?"

"Naw, no' as far as I know, but that cow Mo wouldn't think to tell me anyway, even if she was back."

"You no' getting a bit worried about her? I mean, I told that Stark I thought she'd be round at a pals but that's a while she's been gone. If she was mine..."

"What?" Malky snapped. "So, I don't give a shit, is that it? I can't fuckin win here. No' allowed to have anything to do wi' her but as soon as there's a problem, I'm the bad guy, eh."

"Naw, naw, that's no' what I meant Malky, for fuck's sake, calm down. She'll be fine, if I lived wi' that drunken fuck up for a mother, I'd likely want to get away every now an' again. Do you want another drink?"

"Aye, fine, half and a half."

"Jonny, two half pints of heavy, wi' whisky chasers. Cheers."

The brothers settled into an uneasy truce of silence before resuming their usual banal discussions about football, women and the pros and cons of the current Scottish government's immigration policy.

The pub was poorly patronised these days. The smoking ban hit working class pubs much harder than middle class bistros or food-touting chains, where much of the clientèle were non-smokers anyway. If Scotland's climate had been a little less, er, damp shall we say, it might not have had such a big effect. But, who wants to be forced out into the pissing rain and freezing air of a January evening (or a July one for that matter), when you can sit in your nice, comfy, front room and puff away unmolested by the law?

The next hurdle such pubs needed to overcome was cheap supermarket booze. A single pint served across the counter could be exchanged for about three bottles in one of those multi-pack deals. For people with limited incomes and high tolerances to alcohol, this is a no-brainer. The house beckons again.

The advent of affordable satellite and cable TV services, and huge widescreen televisions to enjoy them upon, removed another thing the pub once had over sitting in the house.

Finally, the dwindling numbers of working class people with jobs, hammered nails into the coffin lids of traditional, characterful pubs all over the country.

Billy and Malky were a dying breed. Driven by habit, bloody-mindedness and nostalgia, they met every Monday afternoon and propped up the bar at the Cross Swords until closing time. The pub had been in the town for years. Locally, it was known as the Cross Words; due to the frequent fights and shouting matches that went on there, as opposed to the punters' penchant for puzzles on the back pages of newspapers.

Being the only two customers present for the majority of those Monday hours was getting more prevalent for the McDuff brothers. It didn't bother them too much but it made playing dominoes a bit boring.

Around nine o'clock, Billy got up and went outside to have a cigarette, leaving Malky to tend his pint, watching the rather dull foreign football match on the television. The bar tapped into some Greek or Turkish satellite system, so the commentary might as well have been in

Swahili, signed for the deaf.

The air was damp, sky cloudy, rain threatening without falling, which was a relief since Billy rarely wore a jacket, let alone carried an umbrella. Sparking up with a cheap, plastic lighter, he inhaled with relish. Smoking since the age of eight, he ignored health warnings, lectures, price hikes or obstacles like smoking bans. Billy liked smoking. Giving up was not an option he ever considered – he was a smoker. End of.

When two lads strolled into the bar with rather more confidence than their tender years might suggest was wise, Billy's trouble radar started transmitting signals. There was just something about them, the look, something his brother would likely take exception to. Especially in the mood he was in tonight. Drawing two, final, resigned puffs on the cigarette before stubbing it out under his toe, Billy pushed open the door, braced himself.

One of the lads lay flat out on the floor, groaning, face leaking blood, otherwise the room was deserted. Jonny Jacobs pointed towards the toilets, resignation and disapproval writ large.

"Sort this out Billy, will you. I don't need any bother from the polis, eh."

"Aye, it's alright Jonny, I'll take care of it."

Billy opened the toilet door to find Malky pummelling fists into the second boy, who was slumped in the metal trough which served as the communal urinal. As the automatic flush kicked in, water sprayed over Malky, who recoiled reflexively.

"Fuck's sake, you've soaked my jeans now, you Polish cunt!" he bellowed at the unconscious youngster, who'd rolled to the floor when Malky let go of him. An entirely superfluous boot to the boy's ribs accompanied his outburst.

"Malky, for Christ's sake, what the fuck happened?"

Wee Malky, never endowed with physical stature, more than made up for this combative shortcoming with speed, power, brutality and reckless abandon. A furious hatred burned in his eyes. This was a look Billy had seen many times before, a look that, on occasion, reduced grown men to quivering wrecks. It represented more than mere hatred of the lad lying prone on the floor; the hatred was for himself, his situation, his parents and all the other people Malky felt had wronged him throughout his life. Every now and again a volcanic plume of frustration, low self esteem and regret would erupt from him, most often manifesting itself in physical violence against others.

"Cheeky Polish wankers! Think they can just swan into my local and order a pint? Naw! You fuckin can't you twats! Should have seen the way this one looked at me."

Malky spat on the boy, leaving a slimy globule of mucus sliding down his cheek. As it happened, the lad on the floor was Latvian but, in Malky's world, anyone with a hint of an Eastern European accent was a job-robbing, benefit-stealing, council-house-waiting-list-jumping, Polish wanker.

"Jesus, Malky, you're going to get the jail again if you keep this up. Jonny will get into bother as well. Come on, let's drag this pair outside and get ourselves away to fuck before one of them calls the law."

The boiling fury reduced to a simmer, the mention of possible incarceration breaking through with surprising effectiveness. Going back inside was not going to happen. He'd die first.

They dragged the two youngsters out into the car park at the back of the pub and then legged it. Not before Malky threw in another couple of kicks of course.

Jonny Jacobs shut up shop early, his only customers now homeward bound or hugging the tarmac out back, and little prospect of any others turning up in the hour and a half before his official closing time. After cleaning up the blood and other spillages, he took a bottle of whisky upstairs to his flat and prepared to welcome oblivion with open arms. It wouldn't be long before his bank manager did the same with the title deeds to his ailing pub.

Malky sat in his chair, flicking through channel after channel on the television, never stopping long on anything in particular, preoccupied, pensive. Even a can of beer failed to capture his attention as it might ordinarily have expected to. It wasn't the earlier altercation with the Baltic interlopers that engaged his thoughts: the message on his mobile phone's answer machine left his mind swirling in dark obsession. Perplexing ideas he knew he shouldn't be entertaining but couldn't resist.

An hour of Stygian brooding later, Malky gulped down the last of his beer, grabbed jacket and keys, and headed out into the now damp night. He needed to clear his head, think.

***

"Right McDuff, spill. My sister says your Ma won the fuckin lottery!"

Cammy McDuff looked at Badger with genuine surprise and incomprehension. "What a load of pish! Who the fuck told her that?"

"Your cousin Tina, eh. Phoned Izzy last night, says her and your Auntie Mo were having a party to celebrate and did she want to come round. My Maw said no chance coz it was about half ten."

"That's just bollocks, Badger. Tina must have been on the glue or something. Do you think I'd be sitting outside in the rain, drinking this pish-water if I was a fuckin millionaire?"

Badger looked around the park and realised Cammy might have a point. Spending the evening in the company of a two litre bottle of cheap cider, half a dozen cigarettes, a solitary joint, drizzling rain and six, wasted teenagers seemed an unlikely choice for someone with enough money to facilitate an alternative arrangement.

"Aye, I heard that an' all Cammy, eh. My wee sister says Tina telt her youse were rich and you'd soon be driving about in a Ferrari or that." piped up Tosh Findlay.

"Honest to fuck. This place is a joke. Folk are so bored they just make shit up!"

"Aye, well, it's all round the scheme. Everybody thinks you're a millionaire!" added Jacko.

"Tell you what McDuff, see if you have won it, and you're no' even buying us a proper carry-out to celebrate, I'll boot your baws!"

Ryan 'Bart' Simpson, self-appointed gang leader and perpetual stirrer of any shit going. "Wouldn't put it past you to keep schtum about that, you tight-fisted wee prick!"

"Aw, fuck off Bart. Who was it bought that fuckin cider then, eh?"

"Aye, thanks a bunch. More money than Bill Gates and all we get is a pishy bottle of cider!"

Bart grabbed the bottle, shaking it up like a winning Formula One driver, soaking Cammy with apple-flavoured froth as the group collapsed into howls of laughter.

Cammy dripped and fumed. He hated Simpson, the egotistical twat; the boy spent most of his free time trying to make Cammy's life a misery. Problem was, he had the fire-power to back up his big gob and big opinions. The only time Cammy ever tried to challenge him, it ended very badly. Now, when derision and humiliation were doled his way in spadefuls, he just took it. He secretly wished his Ma had won the lottery. Money like that would bring him sweet, longed for revenge on that cunt Simpson. He'd arrange for things to happen to him that would make Quentin Tarantino feel squeamish.

If only.

***

Edgars Balodis came to Scotland with high hopes. After Latvia's declaration of independence in 1991, he found himself free to travel like he never was under Soviet rule. He wanted to make a better future for his wife Inese and baby son Juris, escape from poverty and send money home to help others. The West promised riches and freedoms denied him all of his life. He heard the UK, and Scotland in particular, was a place that welcomed foreigners, where hard work would be rewarded and people were friendly.

It took a while for them to settle but, in the end, they forged a decent life for themselves. Another son Andris, came along. They got jobs, they made friends. Edgars became a football coach, the original foreign import. He was good and the boys won, so in that arena at least, most of the prejudice was put to one side.

Juris lay in the hospital bed, tubes and wires connecting his battered body to bleeping, flashing machinery and a bag of fluid on a pole, hypnotically dripping life back into his bloodstream. Edgars stood and looked on as his sobbing wife stroked the hand of their stricken son. Attacked and almost killed for using the wrong pub. A cowardly, racist thug leaving him for dead in the car park along with his friend. Andris sat in the other chair opposite his mother, arms folded, thoughts dark and troubling.

Pete Reynolds was discharged earlier, attacked along with Juris for being a Polish wanker but, in fact, a boy born to Scottish parents in Alloa. His physical injuries were less serious than those sustained by his lifelong pal, Juris, but the mental scars would take a long time to heal.

Edgars was at a loss. He worked hard, he paid his taxes. His boy was a model citizen, studying to be a doctor, contributing, putting something back. Until this moment, Edgars had always thought himself lucky, grateful to the country that changed his family's lives for the better, blessed by God. But this? This was beyond wrong.

Andris stared at the beaten and broken body of his older brother and seethed. Juris looked after him when he was young, when the insults and punches were thrown. As Andris grew up, got stronger, trained in martial arts, he became the protector. Juris; sensitive, clever. He looked at his parents, their anguish riven deep into their faces, and the anger threatened to pop every blood vessel in his head. This was an outrage he would not forgive. Andris stepped out of the room and made his way out to the car park. He lit a cigarette, took out his mobile and punched in the number.

"Pete?"

"Aye, alright Andy?"

"No, I'm not fuckin alright, Pete. Juris is lying in a hospital bed wi' all sorts of wires and tubes sticking out of him, a broken arm and a serious head injury. Who did it?"

"Look, Andy, I know you're raging right now, I would be too if it was my brother, but the guy who did it isn't to be messed wi'."

"Pete, whoever this motherfucker is, he's going to get what's coming to him. Who was it?"

"It was Malky McDuff."

"Oh, brilliant, that arsehole!"

"Aye, the very same. As soon as Juris spoke he just launched himself at us. I was out cold wi' one punch. Never saw it coming and couldn't do anything to help Juris. I know you're a handy cunt yourself Andy, but McDuff's a fuckin headcase, a total radge bastard, eh. You can't go after him. There's his brother Billy to think about an' all. He's nearly as big a fuckin fruit loop as Malky is."

Andris was thinking. Pete was right of course. The McDuffs were the scourge of the estate, notoriety built up over decades. The boy Cammy was another consideration, hung about with a few choice nutters. Taking this lot on would be a huge deal, dangerous.

"Right, well, you leave that with me, Pete. There's no way these fuckers are getting away wi' this. No fuckin way on earth.

"Hang on. Does Billy McDuff's laddie no' play for my Dad's team?"

"Eh, aye, I think he does. Jack isn't it?"

"Aye, that's him. Anyway, as I say, leave it with me and keep your mouth shut. I don't want my Dad worrying about this. Right?"

"Alright Andy, but don't do anything stupid, eh."

10. MISSING INACTION

The letterbox rattled, followed by the dull thump of mail hitting the hall carpet. Billy wandered through to see what postal effluent had been deposited this morning. Junk mail, threatening letters from creditors, bills, and other such irritants were all he could hope for these days. As he approached it became apparent this shitpile was larger than normal. He scooped a few envelopes up, surprised to see two were handwritten. One even had no stamp on it, which was very odd. He opened one and became completely confused by the contents:

Dear Mr and Mrs McDuff,

Please forgive me for sending this letter but I am desperate. My mother is very ill with dementia and needs to go into care but I have just been made redundant and do not have the money to pay for it. I would not normally ask a complete stranger for money but as I say I am desperate and I am hoping you are good people with a sense of compassion for your fellow human being.

Ten thousand pounds sounds like a lot of money but it will make all the difference to us and I hope you can see it in your heart to help my poor, sick mother in her hour of need. If you could send a cheque to the address above, I'd be eternally grateful.

Yours sincerely,

John Brown

A photograph of a frail-looking old woman fell to the floor, he picked it up, trying to work out what was going on. Ten thousand quid? What the hell did this guy think Billy was - a millionaire? Did he think he'd won the lottery or something?

The next letter, almost identical, but sent by a Judy Brown, who appeared to live next door to John: her requirement also for ten thousand pounds but this time to tend to the needs of her frail father, photo enclosed.

The third letter proved tricky to decipher due to the terrible handwriting and spelling but as he read it, the colour drained from Billy, his heart raced.

Billy.

Herd aboot yoor lottery win man. Congrats btw. Sorry tae hassel yoo mate but any chanse yoo cood lend me a few quid tae see me right til ma dole money comes in. I widnay ask but I am desprit.

Hope yoo can help an old pal oot in his hour ay need. For old times sake ay. Ill pay yoo back likes.

Cheers. Davey

His mind whirred. Davey McLatchey lived a few streets away, an occasional drinking buddy and one-time co-worker, back when the Brewery paid both of them a weekly wage. What was he on about? Billy hadn't won the lottery. He checked his numbers on Saturday and, as usual, he'd won precisely fuck all. He looked at the letter, reading and not reading it. Lottery win. If it wasn't him then what about Stella? Surely not? She was still not home and no explanation, no phone call, no text, nothing. Was that why she'd gone missing, because she'd won the lottery? Better not be...if Billy found out the cheating cow had scammed him and the boys out of a fortune, he'd fucking kill her.

Billy was financially illiterate. He didn't have a bank account, a debit card or a credit card. He pestered Stella for cash whenever he needed it and she took care of everything else – bills, council tax, food, clothes for the bairns...everything. He'd never paid for anything beyond his own consumption; ciggies, drink, hash, fast food, trainers.

Billy dumped the rest of the mail on the kitchen counter and called Stella's mobile. It went through to voicemail without ringing: switched off.

"Stella? I don't know what your fuckin game is hen, but you better get your arse back here. I'm getting letters saying we've won the lottery, and begging us for money, eh. Is that right? Have you won the lottery? If you have, I want to know about it, eh. I want my fuckin share! Phone me back or there's going to be bother!"

Stomping upstairs, he got dressed, and poked around the bedrooms. Billy stood with hands on the open doors of his built-in wardrobes, realising that his previous nonchalance regarding Stella's absence may have been unwise. He wasn't the most observant man as far as his wife's garments were concerned, but even he could tell there were gaps on her side of the clothes rail and the only decent suitcase they owned was missing from its place under the bed.

Returning to the living room, he poured himself a straight vodka and necked it. The bottle about a third full. Another couple of similar sized slugs and it'd be empty - how would he replace it? Scrolling through the contacts on his mobile, he reached his brother's number and hit call.

"Malky?"

"Aye. What's happening?"

"Have you heard anything about Stella winning the fuckin lottery?"

"What?"

65

"Stella, has she won the lottery?"

"Fuck's sake Billy, she's *your* wife, how would I know if she's won the fuckin lottery or no'? Why don't you ask *her*?"

"She's gone fuckin AWOL, Malky. Come round the house will you? I've got something I need to show you, eh."

"Right. OK. I'll see you in about half an hour."

***

Stark looked at his new boss with a creeping sense of disdain and dismay.

"A task force?"

"Aye, well, you were probably used to muscling in on the action when you were in that MIT unit in London. Boot's on the other foot now. Price you pay for slumming it with us normal cops, I suppose."

Stark fought the urge to just get up and go. This was exactly what he feared might happen when he made the journey north, effectively demoting himself in the process. The missing girl somehow became important enough to spark the interest and interference of Chief Superintendent Tom Matthews in Stirling. He'd insisted on sending a team from the Regional HQ to help the local yokels out. A show of concern for the well-being of a vulnerable youngster. Reassurance for the populace that something substantial was being done. Stark couldn't help thinking McLaren was amused by his chagrin, delighted even.

"I...we could have handled this ourselves, sir. It's a missing persons case for Christ's sake, no' a serial killer."

"Aye, that's as maybe Stark, but the big man has spoken, so we'll just get on wi' it. DI McGhee's a good lad. He'll be here tomorrow morning. In the meantime, I need to get ready for the press conference wi' the Chief."

"Right, sir."

Stark shut the door behind himself, holding the handle

with a ferocity that left deep indents in his fingers. Without the satisfaction of slamming it, the pressure of his frustration coursed through him, veins in his temple visibly throbbing. He strode down the corridor and crashed into the toilets, letting his enmity roar out.

"Wanker!"

Himself, the DCI, the Chief Super, all three of them? Who knew, but it felt better to have released the valve.

"That's a bit harsh!" A toilet flushed and Ian Barr stepped out from a cubicle, adjusting his belt as he did so. "I try my best you know, sir."

Stark smiled, then gagged as the fumes from the stall wafted toward him.

"Dirty, smelly wanker! That's fuckin bogging you. What did you eat to produce a stench like that?"

Barr grinned, chuckling as he washed his hands. "Kebab and beers, sir. A winning combination, eh."

"Aye, well, it's no' a prize I'd thank you for. I'm off before I pass out or spew up...or both!"

**

"I'm telling you, she's fucked off. No' answering her phone. Not a peep, eh."

Malky, sifting through the pile of letters Billy dumped on the coffee table a few minutes earlier, looked up.

"Do you think she really has won the lottery then? Loads of these scrounging bastards seem to think so."

"Fuck knows, but if she has, she better no' be thinking of running off wi' the money or else, when I catch up wi' her, she'll be very fuckin sorry!"

"Aye, maybe that's where Tina's got to after all. Off spending big bucks wi' her Auntie Stella."

"Could be. Better no' be though. You still no' too worried about Tina then?"

"Nah, she's nearly an adult. She'll have got fed up wi' her Maw an' gone off in the huff. It's no big deal. Anyway, her Maw's made sure I can't have anything to do wi' her, so even if I wanted to help, I'm no' allowed, eh."

Billy decided not to take this line of questioning any further. Malky was never cut out for parenthood. He'd ably demonstrated that on many occasions.

"What I don't get is how come we're getting letters about this. I ken nothing about it but all these fuckers seem to have an inside track."

"Aye, that's a bit weird right enough. I'll ask around, see if anyone else has heard anything, eh."

"Right, fine."

11. FOUND AND LOST

The day drew toward its close, streaks of pink and orange slashing through fading blue. Breeze minimal, rain absent, a gorgeous evening by Scottish standards. Stark walked slowly towards the grave, his mother deep in thought, seemingly oblivious to his approach.

"Hello, Adam," she said without turning to face him. So much for the oblivious theory.

"Hiya, Ma."

As he reached her, he put an arm around her shoulder, kissed her gently on the top of her head. His mother leaned in, sighed.

"Nice to see you, son."

"Aye Ma, I thought you might be up here today. What's that then, seven years since Da went?"

"Aye son, and there's no' a day passes when I don't wish he was still here. Carrie too."

"I know, Ma. Me too."

Standing there, looking down at the headstone, the engravings offered comfort and heartbreak in equal measure. Father and daughter taken from loved ones well before their time. The embers of regret and recrimination began to glow in Stark's gut. He kept his visits here to a minimum. It was just too painful. He placed a small bouquet down on the ground beside his mother's. A tear slipped from his left eye and rolled unhindered down his cheek, dripping onto his lapel. His mother took his hand

and squeezed. A sob rushed out of him without warning and he buried his head in his mother's shoulder. Mary soothed him.

"It's ok, son. I always have a wee bubble when I come here. There's no shame in it. Let it out."

Stark regained his composure. Blowing his nose with a tissue his mother gave him, they headed back to his car. The light faded rapidly once the sun dipped below the horizon and the temperature dipped with it.

"Right then Ma, let's go for a wee bite to eat. I'm paying. We can raise a glass to Dad and Carrie."

"That sounds nice, son. There's an Italian place in the town now. It's nice too. Do you fancy that?"

"Aye, that sounds spot on."

***

Stella McDuff felt good, despite logic trying to remind her she should really be feeling bad. At least a wee bit anyhow. So much about what she'd done since those six little digits flashed up on the television screen could be interpreted as wrong, but shame, remorse and doubt were being held firmly at bay. Her life, up to that moment, consisted of an uninterrupted sequence of bad luck, poor judgement and ill-treatment. In an instant, a whirling conglomeration of random chance converged, changing her life for the better, for ever. She deserved the break, she'd earned it. Nobody was going to take it away from her – not Billy, not Maureen, not anyone.

Stella switched the phone off hours ago. Restoring the power as the train approached the platform at King's Cross, brought forth a clatter of bleeps, a discordant xylophone; texts and voice mails from enraged relatives, studiously ignored. The text from William, cherished.

The train trundled to a halt and the mad scramble to decant began. Stella sat where she was, letting others endure or inflict the sharp elbows, oversized cases, tuts and narrowed eyes. After a few minutes she rose from her seat, retrieved her bag, and headed for the platform unmolested. As soon as she reached the doorway, there he was, her beautiful boy. They embraced, joyful tears flowing. She held his face in both hands and planted several kisses across forehead and cheeks. He squirmed in faux embarrassment – in reality, revelling in this outpouring of maternal affection.

"Oh, Mum, it's so great to see you. But, I can't wait any longer, I'm bursting to know your news and how you managed to convince Dad to let you come down here?"

She smiled, a furtive glance away, then looked back at him.

"Your Da's got no idea where I am, William."

"What? You've left him? Is that your news? Oh my god Mum, please tell me you've finally got away from that bastard?"

"I have, son. I have. Oh, and that's not all."

"What?"

"I've won the lottery."

William's face went through a serious of contortions as his brain tried to process this revelation.

"You've won the lottery? Really? Oh my god! The National Lottery? How much?"

"Six and a half million."

A fleeting moment of silence followed by whooping, screeching, expletives galore, hugging and jumping up and down. Finally, Stella celebrated with genuine joy and relief. Here in London, with the one man in her life she could fully trust, far from past troubles, she felt alive for the first time in her adult life. Rich in every sense of the word.

***

It didn't take much persuading to convince Barr to go for a drink, especially when it transpired Stark would be designated driver.

It'd been an impulse, unplanned. Finishing the meal with his mother, Stark became melancholic, the pressure of guilt weighing heavy. He felt an urge to have company, to talk bollocks about football, distract himself; check out the talent, maybe get laid.

They headed into Stirling, partly because the choice of pubs in Alloa was smaller, and partly because running into your recent collars and would-be clients was no fun. The bar wasn't all that busy as it was a Monday night, even a plethora of cheap drink promotions proving ineffective in persuading folk to partake. Stark wasn't helping much by driving and abstaining, but Barr did his best to make up the shortfall. The lad appeared to be a champion imbiber.

"So, how come you don't drink then, sir?"

"Ach, it's just one of those things. Better off without it. You know?"

"Naw, no' really, sir," said Barr, laughing. "I don't think I could do the teetotal thing like, but fair play to you, eh."

Stark looked around the room and dismissed his chances of succeeding with the maybe get laid part of his plan. Despite the casual tone he deployed, staying dry in a bar was no easier now for Stark than it had ever been. Going so long without drink didn't make the social side of abstaining any easier – especially when he was with blokes who were getting smashed. Distraction, change of subject.

"So, what's your story then, Ian? You're married right?"

"Aye, to Kirsty. Been together seven years, married four."

"Kids?"

Barr looked away, coughed, slugged his rapidly diminishing pint.

"Naw."

Stark could see pain etched on his new colleague's face.

"Sorry man, I wasn't..."

"Naw, it's alright, sir. We've been trying for a couple of years. Kirsty has some women's issues. Spent a fuckin fortune on that IVF but it's no' worked, eh. I'm no' too bad wi' it. If it's no' to be then so be it, but she's no' coping all that well wi' it likes."

"Ah, sorry to hear that, Ian. These things can be weird mind, folk are convinced it's never going to happen then, out the blue, they get preggers. You never know."

Barr shrugged, drained the last of his pint, and an awkward silence ensued. Stark wished he'd never asked the bloody question, stuck to bollocks about football as originally planned. Some horrible R&B number was being vomited from the sound system, not old school 1960's R&B, some modern pish that passed itself off as music but as far as Stark was concerned, amounted to little more than a drum machine and somebody yowling along to it like a copulating cat. It wasn't helping to lighten the mood.

"D'you want another one?"

"Actually sir, do you mind if we call it a night? Sorry, but I've probably had enough for a school night and we're going to be busy the morra looking for Tina McDuff, eh."

"Aye no worries, Ian. Let's go."

After dropping Barr off, Stark drove back to his Mum's house. He parked in the mono-block driveway listening to *The Bends*, letting Thom Yorke's soaring performance on *Sulk* act like an aural pan of water, drenching those over amorous felines from the bar earlier.

Sitting there, headlights off, waiting to go into the house, Stark thought about how odd it felt. Like being back at Tulliallan doing his basic training. He wondered what he'd have done if he had scored in the bar. Back in the day, he'd be happy to park up in a secluded spot, recline the seat and go for it. Nowadays, if he tried that, he might end up with an audience and a starring role in some internet download. A bad back to boot no doubt.

If he took anyone inside, he couldn't have done the deed with his Ma a few feet down the hall, and he doubted any woman would be too impressed by such domestic arrangements at his age – temporary situation or not.

Getting his own place needed to come up the agenda of things to get sorted. His Ma was great, her cooking epic, but he needed to knock about the house in the buff, scratch his balls in front of the TV, play music too loud, leave the toilet reeking without trace of self consciousness or a scramble for air freshener, fail to clean up after himself for days on end. Be a single bloke. As Thom and the boys broke in to *Street Spirit* he resolved to start looking for somewhere the next morning.

***

Greg Marshall stared at the computer screen, willing the right words to appear. Every instinct screamed at him to stop this, forget it. Pointless, humiliating, never going to work. But, he had to, for Brandon.

For over a year, every passing day had carried away a little bit of hope. A relentless, ruthless clock, ticking down the time his precious son had left. It would cost a fortune to go to the USA for the stem cell treatment and, so far, the generosity of friends and family, boundless though it seemed, barely dented the required amount.

Yes, they were scum, and no, he'd never normally take anything to do with the likes of them. But they were all he had. Even they must understand his desperation, his need. They had kids of their own. How would they feel? Kirsty was right; likely just a tall tale, an embellished half-truth, but he had nothing to lose.

Fingers began to move, trance-like translation of feelings flowing onto the empty page, gradually filling it with a suggestion of hope.

A chance taken, a dice rolled, his own lottery ticket filled out.

***

Stella lay in bed in William's spare room – full stomach,

full heart. The room, tastefully spartan, spotlessly clean; just what she'd have expected.

The mobile phone sat on the bedside table. All evening she'd studiously ignored it, switched off again, buried in her bag. Now, charging; blinking, green light beckoning, imploring. She picked it up, ignoring anything with Billy's name attached to it but drawn to the text messages from Maureen. What she read made her mouth desiccate and her stomach do a forward roll, without having the decency to wait for the rest of her body to catch up. Tina missing...Maureen frantic. This changed the game entirely.

She hoped to escape from Billy by holing up in London with William – initially at least. She always intended to see Maureen, Tina and the boys right for money but from a distance, to avoid face to face unpleasantness. Billy, Malky and a host of others would thrust grasping, ungrateful and unworthy hands toward her if they knew where she was or how much she'd won. Stella couldn't rule out the possibility of violent extortion or blatant theft on the part of the brothers; she desperately wanted to avoid giving either of those bastards a penny.

This was typical. Why couldn't God just cut her a break? She'd been so grateful to Him for answering her prayers to win the money in the first place. Now, He seemed determined to take it off her again. She went to church, she prayed, she went to confession regularly, absolved herself of those minor indiscretions it was designed to expunge from the record. Of course, she wasn't a saint, but who was? What had she done to deserve His contempt?

The choices narrowed down to one possibility. No choice. She'd have to go back, support Maureen, help find Tina. Maybe the money would prove useful? A reward, a private detective, something, anything.

Stella got up and went through to the lounge. William, curled up on the sofa, watching television, looked up as she walked into the room.

"Alright, Mum? Can't sleep?"

"I've got a bit of a problem, son."

"How, what's up?"

"It's Tina, she's gone missing. I need to go back and be wi' your Auntie Maureen."

"But Mum, if you go back, Dad's going to be furious. Who knows what he might do!"

"I ken that son, but I can't just leave my sister to it when her wee lassie's gone missing."

William stood, walked over to his drinks cabinet and mixed up two large gin and tonics.

"Ok, I can see why you'd want to help Auntie Mo, but we need a plan. You can't just shoot straight back up there. Sit down, have a drink and let's think this through."

12. BURNT OFFERINGS

"Report of a disturbance down the Bottom End, sir."

Stark was disorientated, caught out by the sudden chiming of his mobile at such an early hour. The sultry voice of the young, female PC made it feel like some weird, erotic dream rather than a call to action.

"Fire and ambulance are already in attendance. The first of our guys down there just called in for assistance, sir."

Stark swung his legs out of bed as the PC relayed more details to him. "Ok, thanks. I'll get dressed and head down there now."

He assembled as coherent an outfit as his brain would allow while only half awake. As he did so, he heard his mother padding toward his room.

"Everything alright, son?"

"Aye, it's fine, Ma. Got a call out. Just you go back to bed."

"Do you want a flask or a wee sandwich to take wi' you?"

Such a typical Mary gesture.

"Naw, thanks anyway, Ma. I'll be fine. I need to go, I've no' got time for all that."

"Where's the fire?"

"Well, funnily enough."

Stark drove back into town. He knew the scheme well,

despite his long absence, but even without such previous, it wasn't hard to find his intended destination. Smoke and flames billowed from the upper windows of a maisonette, which seemed as though it might be fortified in some way. Two fire engines and an ambulance in attendance, red and blues jabbing at the darkness. A crowd of onlookers gesticulated, bayed obscenities in the general direction of the house, held back by a plucky foursome of uniformed cops and a couple of firemen. The remainder of the fire crews tried to deal with the conflagration.

Stark approached Barr who'd arrived before him.

"What's the script, Ian?"

"That's Graham Connelly's house, sir."

"Who's he?"

"Paedo. Been the focus of a lot of bad feeling down here since they let him out the jail and housed him there. My missus has been getting a lot of grief over it."

"Great. Looks like that bad feeling's spilled over into something a bit more serious. Why would your missus get grief then, she on the council or work wi' probation?"

"Naw, she's a social worker, sir. Everybody thinks anything like that is to do wi' her, whether it is or it isn't."

"Aye, scapegoats are usually a lot easier to come by than a sense of perspective in these situations."

They donned stab vests, gloves and hats. A van rolled up carrying reinforcements. About ten suited and booted officers piled out, running to the aid of their beleaguered colleagues.

"We'll let the cavalry do the dirty stuff, Barr. No point messing up a good pair of troosers unless I really need to."

Stark became aware of his own voice, the returning colloquial informality. Comfy shoes back on.

"Ok sir, sounds like a plan to me. To be fair though, I hope they troosers aren't your good ones, eh."

Stark looked down at the track suit bottoms, chucked on in his haste to get out the door, and couldn't help but laugh.

"Cheeky bastard! These are designer I'll have you know. Best of gear!"

It took a few minutes for a greater degree of order to be attained, allowing the fire guys to complete the job of dousing the flames. It didn't improve the crowd's mood or decrease their animosity toward the occupant of the house. It seemed fairly obvious they were hoping Graham Connelly was home and crisping nicely, as opposed to out somewhere, oblivious to all this burning hatred.

Stark approached the Fire Sub Officer on duty.

"How are you doing, mate? Under control now is it?"

"I think so. Need to let it cool down a bit before we let anyone go in for a look though. You new then?"

"Aye, sorry, DI Adam Stark."

They shook hands.

"SO Frankie Boyle. Aye, like the comedian, and naw, I can't tell you a joke."

"Err, right then Frankie, no bother. Do we know if anyone was home?"

"Not for definite. It's that paedo Connelly's house. Can't say I'd lose any sleep if he was in there."

"Aye, DC Barr was telling me about him when we arrived. I take it we're looking at arson?"

"More than likely given the nature of the beast involved. We'll know for definite once the investigators have been able to get in there and have a proper look."

"How about the neighbours? Everyone accounted for?"

"Aye, there's an old woman lives on the ground floor. She made it out fine. Been taken to hospital suffering from shock but otherwise she's unharmed, eh."

"Ok, that's good."

As much as he might empathise with Boyle's ill will or the actions of the lynch mob, maintaining a professional distance mattered. A crime was a crime. Allowing an attitude of 'he deserved it' to dominate proceedings might let something crucial slip the net. Dangerous, morally questionable people set house fires and barbecued other human beings – regardless of their victim's credentials. The recklessness meant innocent bystanders could get hurt. Vigilante justice was nothing of the sort, otherwise why have a police force, courts, and due process in the first place?

"Alright, while we're waiting for it to cool off, we'll go and have a word wi' a few of the crowd and see if any of them know anything."

"Good luck wi' that, DI Stark. You've got more chance of getting them to hand over tenners than help you find who torched this place."

Twenty minutes later, this seemed like a fairly accurate summation of the attitude of the onlookers. Most of them made a sharp exit or refused point blank to cooperate. Those who did offer an opinion seemed to think whoever was responsible deserved a medal rather than a court appearance. The list of possible suspects would be lengthy.

"Oh, that's just magic, the Chief is going to love this. We'll get it in the neck from the bleeding hearts about protecting him better *and* the Daily Mail brigade who think we should've strung him up in the first place. Have we any idea if Connelly was in there?"

"No, sir. I'm going back down there in a bit to have a look around. Fire guys told us to wait for it to cool down and let them do some safety checks."

DCI McLaren sat forward in his seat, and pinched his fingers together across his forehead.

"Ok, let me know how you get on."

"What about DI McGhee, sir? Is he no' due here soon? Do you want me to wait and talk to him before I go?"

"Oh aye, so he is. Em, no, it's ok. I'll fill him in on the situation wi' the McDuff lassie. You get on wi' finding out what's happened to the paedo. As if anyone actually cares."

Stark knew what he meant. A jibe, a belittlement.

McLaren pushing him toward the unwelcome task of finding justice for a reviled child molester while DI McGhee rides in like a white knight and finds the missing girl. Just had to suck it up. Always going to be rough to begin with. Whining would only make things worse, prove to his detractors he was up himself or incapable or both.

"Ok sir. I'll let you know how I get on."

"Right."

The DCI was already on the phone to McGhee, waving Stark away without even looking at him.

Fucking wanker.

***

Funny how something as simple as going to the supermarket could save your life. Not metaphorically in the '*Thank god you've got some milk, I'm choking for a cup of tea. You've saved my life*!' kind of way. Literally, as in the '*Someone just set fire to my house hoping I was in it, but I was out buying milk, as I was choking for a cup of tea. You've saved my life*!' kind of a way.

Graham Connelly rounded the corner and stopped: a ferocious rabble wishing him dead, cheering on the destruction of his temporary lodgings. Luckily, it was dark, he was disguised and the majority of people had their backs to him.

He couldn't move. His trophies, his mementos – the ones they didn't know he had - going up in flames. A chunk of his spirit spiralled skywards with the smoke and sparks. Connelly wanted to run into the heart of the fire and rescue them. Either that or die trying. But, he couldn't move. He'd never make it anyway, the mob would tear him apart as soon as they saw through his flimsy camouflage.

Only the McDuffs would do this. Only they maintained enough bile and determination to go this far. Connelly pulled his collar up, thrust hands into pockets and forced himself to walk away.

According to some fish-wife gossip overheard in the shop earlier, the McDuffs were lottery winners. Good for them, good for nothing. However, all the money in the world couldn't settle his bill. For now, the caravan would be his hideout, provide time to regroup, recover his nerve. He needed to replace his souvenirs and he knew just where to start collecting again.

13. BROKEN

"Bold as fuckin brass, she just walked in the door this morning, eh. No sorry, no how are you Ma, nothing."

"You should just be happy she's back, Maureen. Thankful nothing terrible happened to her."

Maureen didn't know it but Tina recently acquired a new boyfriend and that's where she'd spent the last two nights. An older guy with money and a job. Maureen wouldn't have approved the sleepover if Tina had asked. She didn't want him finding out her real age.

"Aye, well, that's as maybe Stella but she's caused a total shitstorm. The school are going to go mental. I even had to go crawling to the filth for help. Had to deal wi' that prick Adam Stark."

"Adam Stark? What, that used to live near us when we were kids?"

"Aye, that's the one. Been transferred back to Alloa from London, apparently."

"Unlucky!"

"Aye, very good Stella, doll. But, even if it wasn't that dickhead, you know how keen I am on the polis at the best of times. Turns out she'd been wi' some pal I didn't ken, getting pissed. She says it was a spur of the moment thing. Didn't think it was a big deal. Didn't think I'd be that bothered. She claims her phone ran out of charge an' she left the charger in her room, that's how she didn't phone me to let me ken. She's a stupid, selfish, wee cow. I've no idea where she gets her attitude from, eh."

Stella bit her tongue.

"Anyway, that's all well and good Stella, but what the fuck is going on wi' you? Where are you an' when are you coming back?"

Stella felt torn. Should she let Maureen know where she was. She could be such a blabbermouth but she wanted to trust her sister, wanted to let her know she was ok, that things would work out fine.

"I'm in London...and...I'm no' coming back, Maureen."

"What? You've got to be fuckin joking! What about the boys, an' Billy, an' me, eh? He'll fuckin kill you if you don't come back, Stella. You do know that don't you?"

"He'll no' touch me if he can't find me. You need to keep quiet about this an' help me. I'm sick of being treated like dirt by him and they ungrateful wee shites. I'll see you an' the boys right, but I'm staying here in London."

"You're off you're head, Stella. Billy will never let you piss off wi' all that money. He'll find you an' he'll kill you. And, I don't mean give you a doing, I mean actually put you six feet under!"

Stella wasn't really cut out for this life on the run. The idea of spending the rest of her life looking over her shoulder, waiting for Billy to track her down, didn't appear glamorous or exciting but she needed to brazen it out for now. Act the part.

"Listen, Maureen, I've got the money an' the time to make sure he never finds me but I need your help. Just say nothing for now, eh. I'll put a wad of cash in your bank if you give me the details, an' you can go round an' give some of it to Billy. That should mean the boys get fed an' watered at least. Right?"

There was a long pause at the other end of the line before a hefty sigh.

"Ok, but I'm no' happy about it, Stella. You should come home. You don't belong in London, you're an Alloa lassie. Just come back an' ask for a divorce. Christ, it's no' as if you can't afford a lawyer, eh."

"Look, Maureen, will you help me or no'?"

"Aye, you're my big sister, of course I'll help you."

"Right, so give me your bank details."

***

The Fire Investigation Officer confirmed Connelly's house was set ablaze deliberately. Traces of accelerant and the pattern of the fire indicating someone pushed a burning rag or paper through the letterbox. Temperatures inside never reached the levels required to incinerate a body, so the absence of Connelly's charred remains suggested he was elsewhere when the building went up. The flat itself was gutted; none of Connelly's possessions appeared to have survived, even if he had.

Stark stood outside the block and looked around. Small numbers of people went about their business, some of them stopping to stare for a few seconds before losing interest and moving on. Drops of rain began to splat onto the pavement then, in a sudden rush, the sky tipped huge quantities of liquid earthward. Stark and Barr dived for cover in their car.

"Bloody hell, sir, that came out of nowhere."

"Aye, if there's one thing this country does well, Barr, it's rain."

They watched and listened, temporarily transfixed as the water cascaded down.

"So, what do you think, sir?" said Barr, breaking the spell.

"What? Oh, aye, the case? I'm no' sure it's going to turn out to be the butler, in the pantry, wi' the rolling pin, do you?"

Barr grinned in approval.

"More like the Ned, down the Bottom End, wi' the oily rag, sir."

"The problem is, Barr, there's going to be a list of folk

as long as the electoral roll that could be implicated in this. I'll be fuckin amazed if anybody wants to volunteer any info either."

"What about Connelly, sir? Has he been in contact wi' anyone yet?"

"Naw, I spoke to his probation officer and he's no' heard anything from him. Neither has his psychologist, apparently."

"Does he have any relatives to ask for help?"

"No' sure. It's the kind of thing even a mother would find hard to forgive. Chances are he's on his own."

"Aye, right enough, sir."

Stark thought about how he might feel if it turned out a convicted child molester was living in his neighbourhood. The demonstrations of anger and reproach the previous night were nothing to do with demographics or income brackets. Just as fierce, if not fiercer, objections would come from a middle-class scheme elsewhere in the town. Alloa folk were the same as any other folk when it came to protecting their kids. Stark was thankful he didn't have to make decisions about such things, he just helped tidy the mess up afterwards.

"Anyway, the best we'd be doing wi' this now is criminal damage, arson or the like. I'm no' convinced the boss will want to pursue it unless Connelly appears an' makes a complaint. Saying that, it's a council house, so I reckon it'll go no further than an insurance claim. Let's go back to the station, write this up and see what other mischief we can get up to instead."

Stark felt his mobile vibrate in his pocket. The call was from DCI McLaren. He toyed with cancelling it but his professionalism kicked in.

"Yes, sir?"

"Stark, just to let you know that Tina McDuff has turned up safe and well. Her mother says she came home this morning after a couple of days at a friend's house."

"So, DI McGhee? Is he away back to Stirling then?"

Stark found it hard not to snigger.

"Aye, it's bloody ridiculous! I've a good mind to charge the wee bitch wi' wasting police time. Anyway, she's fine, so just letting you know."

"Ok, sir. Thanks. Nothing much to report from here. As suspected, it's arson, but no dead body, so Connelly's still safe and no' well in the head."

"Ha! Aye, very good, Stark. Still, at least we'll no' have the nationals descending on us. Nothing like a dead paedo and a lynch mob to get readership figures up."

"Aye, that's true, sir. Me and Barr will be back in a bit. Going to try a few neighbours, see if anyone saw anything. I'm no' holding my breath as far as that goes mind."

"Fine, box ticked, process followed. Don't take too long though, not what I'd call a top priority."

"No, me neither, sir."

That's why you've dumped it on me you disingenuous bastard.

***

Lying in bed, sleep refusing to take him, Stark stared up at the ceiling; thoughts jumping between disparate, unconnected subjects. The red, digitized numerals of his bedside clock taunted him with the lateness of the hour.

He heard his mother get out of bed, shuffle toward the bathroom. Light flooded the hallway briefly as she flicked the switch but darkness returned as the door closed. The lock clicked, followed swiftly by retching. A violent, copious, unsettling bout of vomiting ensued. Stark felt his breathing become shallow, erratic, his entire attention centred on the events unfolding a few metres away. How many times must his Ma have been the one on the outside of a toilet door listening to him spew? As a kid, when illness or dodgy ingestion could be blamed, or later, when alcohol became part of his social life. It was odd, unnerving even, to be listening to his Mum take his place. Mary rarely got ill. When all around her were dropping like flies, overcome by flu or chickenpox or norovirus, Mary would be tending to the sick, never succumbing herself. It actually made him nauseous to listen to this.

Eventually, she stopped. The toilet flushed, taps turned on and off, the door opened, the escaping light extinguished. As Mary returned to her room, Stark swung his legs over the side of his bed and sat up. Should he go to her? Something was wrong, something more than a dodgy oyster was at work here, he could sense it. That wan look Mary had been sporting the past few days, the lack of spark and zip. A tightness in his jaw began to build, his stomach fluttered. Fear nagged at him.

He got up and put on his dressing gown – a hideous garment he'd never have worn in the privacy of his own house. Softly knocking at his mother's door, he poked his head around it.

"Ma, are you ok?"

Mary, who'd been facing away from him on her side, rolled onto her back.

"Aye, I'm ok, son. Just been a wee bit sick. Must have been something I ate, eh."

Stark stepped into the room and sat on the edge of her bed.

"What have you had to eat the day then?"

"Aw, no' that much, don't worry about it, son. You go back to bed. I'll be fine. A good night's sleep will be just the ticket. Same for you. No doubt you need to get up early for work."

He reached out, patted her hand. Stark felt the bones, the papery skin, but most of all the cold. The fear swept in again like a front from the North Atlantic.

"You sure you're ok? You've been looking a wee bit peaky last few days."

Mary was touched and upset. She hated lying to her son. Well, lying was a bit strong, more like withholding information. Then again, he was a policeman, that sort of thing might count as illegal, as good as lying to him. She would tell him. But not yet.

"Aye, I'm fine, son. Now, off you go. See you at breakfast."

Reluctantly, he stood.

"Ok, Ma. Night night."

"Night night, sleep tight."

"Don't let the bed bugs bite!" they said in unison and chuckled. An old favourite they hadn't used in years.

Stark went back to bed but sleep took a long time to come.

14. CONFLICTING VIEWS

Malky and Billy's combined fortune amounted to about three pounds twenty. The kitchen had been stripped of all the items that required four minutes in a microwave, could be heated (cremated) in a frying pan or eaten raw. They were out of milk and bread. Most importantly, they were dangerously low on cigarettes and a single bottle of beer kept a lonely vigil in the fridge.

The place looked like a bomb had gone off, leaving the human inhabitants standing but throwing all their possessions into the air and scattering them around. Clothes, pots, crockery and cutlery lay where they fell, mostly unwashed.

"This isn't funny, Malky. Where the fuck is she and how am I supposed to get by wi' three quid?"

His brother shrugged as the day's mail hit the hall carpet.

"Oh, let me guess, more fuckin begging letters! What a fuckin sick joke that is. It's me that needs to do some begging."

Malky wandered over to the pile of mail, absently flicked through the envelopes one by one.

"Look, don't worry about these scrounging bastards, I'll sort them out."

The doorbell clanged and Malky answered it.

"Oh, brilliant. What the fuck do you want?"

"From you? Fuck all. It's Billy I've come to see."

"What's happening wi' Tina? Is she home yet?"

Mo sneered and shook her head. "Oh, right, so suddenly you give a shit do you? No' that you actually care but aye, she's home safe an' sound. Now let me in, I need to give Billy a message, eh."

Malky stood aside, fists clenched in anger. Mo walked into the lion's den, holding a carrier bag full of cold, hard cash.

"Jesus, Billy, look at the state of this place! Where are the boys?"

Billy walked through from the kitchen, dark malevolence casting a pall over him.

"They're at school, no' that it's got anything to do wi' you. If you've come here to gloat or start up wi' some shite or other, then I suggest you get the fuck out, before I fuckin lose it."

Mo held the bag up at arms length, inverted it and shook the contents out.

"A present from Stella."

Billy and Malky stood open mouthed, disbelieving. Mo took her chance to bolt. The slam as she left broke the trance. Billy exploded.

"Malky, get after that bitch! I want to know what the fuck is going on!"

The two men raced for the door, arriving simultaneously, thus hindering each other's ability to grasp the handle and get out into the garden. They made it to the path too late. Mo, disappearing up the street in a taxi, high-tailing it away from the powder keg of wrath she'd just lit the fuse for.

The keg went up in spectacular style. After an expletive-strewn rant, Billy and Malky went back inside. They looked at the piles of twenty and ten pound notes lying amongst the detritus of their domestic ineptitude with something akin to distrust.

"How much *is* that?"

"I've no idea. Looks a lot though."

"You know what this means, Billy?"

"What?"

"Stella did win the lottery. You're a fuckin millionaire bro, a fuckin millionaire!"

Malky started to laugh maniacally, throwing money in the air, kissing piles of notes. Billy grabbed him by the shoulders and brought his celebration to an abrupt halt.

"Malky, *I'm* no' a fuckin millionaire, that thieving cow Stella is, eh. There's no way I'm going to let her, or that scheming, alky, bitch of a sister get away wi' this, man. No fuckin way on earth."

"I hear you, bro. In the meantime, let's go down the pub and get a pint. It'll help us work out what the fuck we're going to do."

"Aye Jonny, it's right enough, Stella won the lottery and we're millionaires."

The barman shook his head and whistled, slowly turning the bar towel around the inside of a glass and then placing it on the rack under the counter.

"Bloody hell, Billy, I've never met a millionaire before. What's it like being stinking, filthy rich?"

"Fuckin brilliant, you peasant!"

The three men laughed, Billy and Malky chinked glasses together.

Over the next few hours drink flowed, inebriation advanced. As was so often the way these days, they were the only customers. However, their new found wealth meant Jonny actually made a good profit from them. The first decent takings all week. That very morning he'd received a letter from the bank threatening him with action if he didn't sort out the late payments on his overdraft and mortgage. A problem he kept ignoring. Fingers in ears, not listening, shouting la, la, la.

Jonny Jacobs once made his living as a professional footballer. When his playing days came to an end, he invested in the pub and grafted to make it a success. For many years it did fine, but the recent economic climate, the smoking ban, and a habit of backing horses that were allergic to winning, took his finances into freefall.

And now, here he stood, the bank's axe about to decapitate years of sweat and toil, keeping the company of a couple of work-shy, violent, no-hopers who, thanks to sheer blind luck, were rolling in cash. Where was the justice in that?

"I tell you what lads, thank fuck you're spending in here coz no other fucker appears to be."

"Aye, you're no' awfy busy these days JJ are you?"

"Naw Billy, it's tough times for the likes of me. Folk just sit in their houses watching telly an' drinking carry-outs from the supermarket."

Malky's face was stony as he sipped his latest pint.

"Well, me and Malky like the pub, JJ. Always have, eh. You can count on us. Is that no' right, Malky?"

"Aye," said Malky. Flat and emotionless.

"Right, I'm going out for a puff. Back in a minute."

Billy slipped off his stool and swayed out into the street.

Malky stopped staring into his pint, looked up at Jonny with naked aggression.

"On your uppers are you, Jonny?"

"Well, it's pretty bad, Malky. Got a threatening letter from the bank this morning. Have to hope things will get better but I'm no' holding my breath."

"Do you think I'm buttoned up the fuckin back, Jonny?"

"What?"

"You heard me. Do you reckon I'm some kind of wanker?"

Jonny's nerves crackled in warning. The red mist was cloaking Malky and he'd seen what that meant too often to be anything other than unsettled by it.

"Naw, of course no', Malky. You and Billy are good customers. My best customers. What's up wee man?"

Malky stood, grabbed two handfuls of Jonny's shirt and hauled him half way across the bar leaving their faces a couple of inches apart.

"Whoa, Malky, fuck's sake mate. Take it easy."

"Take it fuckin easy? You think I can't see what the fuck you're up to? You're angling for money, taking advantage of my brother's better nature. Well, let me put you right Jonny-boy. You're getting fuck all. Not a fuckin bean. Do we understand each other?"

"I don't know what you're on about, Malky. I wasn't after money. Billy just asked me how things were."

"After you set him up for it more like."

With unexpected speed and strength, Malky dragged Jonny bodily over the counter and down onto the floor of the bar. The older man thumped to the ground, all the wind knocked from him. The younger man leant in close.

"Let me make things crystal for you, Jonny. We are the McDuffs. We don't take shit from anybody. You're no' getting our money an' neither is any other scrounging cunt from round here. I don't care about your sob story, it's no' my fuckin problem. Don't ever mention money to me again or you're going to have a lot more to worry about than the fuckin bank manager. You got it?"

Jonny nodded.

"Aye, I've got it, Malky."

"Good. You better have."

Malky let go of the shirt, stood and returned to his stool. Jonny got to his feet, rubbing the back of his head, rolling his shoulders, trembling like a new-born lamb. Returning to his station behind the counter, he jammed a glass up against the optic attached to the bottle of Dalwhinnie - his favourite single malt - allowing the amber liquid to refill its measure in the apparatus before repeating the exercise. A double nippy sweetie. Burning and soothing, gliding down his throat like warm honey, returning hyperactive synapses to a state akin to normal.

The door swung open and Billy returned to the bar, the

remnants of his smoke sneaking back in with him.

"Same again, Malky?"

His brother nodded, eyeballing Jonny as he did so.

"And have one for yourself, JJ."

"Naw, it's alright, Billy."

"Pish man, take a drink! I can afford it, eh!"

Jonny's laughter was as empty as his bank account.

Andris Balodis watched and waited. They'd been in the pub for a long time and must have consumed a huge amount of alcohol by now. This was good. This gave him an edge, helped even the odds a little. The older brother, Billy, liked to smoke, appearing twice as often outside the pub as Malky did. The temptation to exact his revenge every time the cowardly animal sparked up intense, but resisted. Getting himself arrested or, worse still, jailed, would help no-one.

Somebody told him these low-lives had won the lottery. An absolute fortune. Somehow, it made things worse, made him even angrier, more determined than ever to retaliate. But, Andris possessed a precious commodity in such circumstances – time. He would be patient, wait for the perfect moment, deliver his retribution with relish and gusto.

***

"Stella, please come home, eh."

"Look, Maureen, I told you, I can't come home. Billy would fuckin kill me and to be honest I wouldn't blame him. If he'd won the lottery and then buggered off, I'd be pretty pissed off an' all."

"Aye, that's as maybe, but you could give him a pile of money to leave you alone and then just buy your own house and everything would be hunky dory."

"It's no' going to be that easy though is it, eh? He's a fuckin bampot. The first time he gets pissed, he'll be round my new house wi' a baseball bat, and before you know it, I'll be in the hospital...or worse. Naw, I can't come home, Maureen. It's a shame, but that's just the way it is."

"What about the laddies though? Billy's a useless bastard when it comes to looking after the house. They'll be living in a pigsty, Christ, when I went around to drop that money off, it was already in a right state, and that was only after a few days. You can't just abandon them, you're their Ma!"

Stella could see what Maureen was trying to do - ratchet up the guilt, stir those maternal instincts. But, she also realised this was more to do with Maureen, about her share of the money, her chance to escape the scheme, than about worries for the boys' welfare. Whatever the motive, it was working, Stella's guilty conscience broke out like a nasty rash; itching, irritating, failing to respond to cursory scratching. She shouldn't harbour such negative feelings for her own children. Billy represented all that was really wrong with her life. She could have taken the pill if she'd been prepared to ignore the Pope's guidance, or faked illness to explain a lack of fertility, or refused sex more often. The boys didn't ask to be borne or born. Stella was complicit in their making and their development. As much as it might suit her to lay all the blame for any inadequacies at Billy's door, the unavoidable truth was that she contributed. Maybe not fifty per cent but contributed nonetheless. Maureen was right, Stella shouldn't leave their future in Billy's inadequate hands. Providing him with piles of money would not result in a better life for the kids. He was useless, disorganised, wouldn't know how to pay a bill or even buy a week's groceries. They'd be the first kids of a millionaire to be taken into care due to neglect. She shouldn't let that happen, she wouldn't let that happen.

"What do you mean, a right state?"

"Dirty dishes, empty cans, full ashtrays lying everywhere. The place was a pure midden!"

Maureen sensed victory. She could rely on Stella

responding to emotional blackmail, a guilt trip. Her big sister was a soft touch, too sensitive. Maureen didn't mind exploiting this weakness, if it made Stella come back. Anyway, what would Stella spend all that money on if she didn't give some of it to her? It was ridiculous, unthinkable that she would move to London and become some kind of snobby, posh bird. She was Alloa born and bred, working class and proud. A big house in the town and a chance to stick one right up all those judgemental bastards looking down their noses; that was all she needed. All either of them needed.

"Can you no' help out Maureen, go round and tidy up, make the bairns some dinner and that?"

"Stella, you ken fine me and Billy hate each other's guts. He's already raging about me dumping that money on his living room floor. What do you think he might do if I swan up telling him I'm there to clean his house and feed his weans? I've had to move out of my house so he can't come over and kick up fuck about where you are. In fact, that's another reason you need to come back. I can't stay here forever, eh."

"Where are you staying then?"

"One of them travel lodges on the outskirts of the town. He'll find out though, and when he does, it's no' going to be pretty. That wee bastard Malky will no doubt get involved an' all."

Stella's scratching might soon draw blood.

"Oh, for God's sake Maureen, lay it on a bit thicker why don't you? I've put up wi' that bastard for the past twenty years and now, when I finally get a chance to break free, you're making me feel as guilty as sin about it."

"Look, Stella, it's no' my fault, eh. I'm no' the millionaire in hiding. I told you he would go mental if I took that money round there and, true to form, he went totally radge. You need to come back and help me sort this out, get rid of the useless prick, and start a new life here, wi' your family an' proper friends by your side."

Stella's head swam but her sister's logic was inescapable. This stupid plan to run away wasn't a plan at all, just stupid. In fact, she'd probably made things worse rather than better. Billy was a first class headcase when riled and she couldn't think of anything that would rile him more than what she'd done. Terror and indecision clamped her in a bear hug which threatened to squeeze all the life out of her.

"Maureen, I can't talk about this any more, eh. I need to think, make some decisions, think about how to deal wi' Billy, without getting both our heads kicked in. I'll call you later ok?"

"Aye, ok. Cheerio the now."

"Right, cheerio."

Stella disconnected the call and laid the phone on the arm of the couch in William's flat. The enormity of the mess she'd made smashed her in the face like a brick. Self pity streamed as she buried face in hands.

William stood in the hallway, contemplating his next move. He could see how much this situation was tearing Stella up. They may have been a pair of unpleasant, ungrateful turds, but despite all their shortcomings, she loved his brothers. There had to be a way to make sure his other parent's bully boy tactics didn't win the day. He walked into the room, sat down beside his mother and hugged her.

"Don't worry Mum, we'll sort this, you'll see. Everything's going to be ok."

***

Billy and Malky were both mightily pissed up. The conversation du jour revolved around how they were going to extract more money from Stella and, in Malky's case in particular, get their own back on Maureen for the stunt with the bag of dosh. The more they drank, the more violent and extreme their revenge fantasies became.

"I tell you Billy, that cow's had it coming for years, eh. She's treated me like shit, kept my wee lassie from me by telling fuckin lies to the polis, an' fleeced me for maintenance money."

A distinct distortion of the truth. Billy knew it, but embellished detail aside, the crux of it rang true.

"Right, Malky, let's go back to the house. I'll get us a few cans from the Offy and we can work out exactly how we're going to deal wi' that pair of scheming bitches.

"Jonny-boy, we're out of here mate, see you later."

The still-shaken landlord waved, avoiding eye contact with Malky; blazing, daring him to rise to the bait.

Out in the street, both men felt their already addled senses take a further pounding from the fresh air.

"Jesus, I am fuckin blootered, bro."

"Aye, me an' all, Billy."

"Ok, maybe we should just forget the carry out?"

"What? You some kind of nancy boy, like that laddie of yours?"

As soon as the last of the words were across his lips, Malky knew they'd also crossed a line. One he usually avoided. The haymaker from Billy, although poorly executed, still sent him tumbling as it glanced off the side of his head. A full connection would have spread his nose from ear to ear.

"Don't you ever fuckin mention him again! Right?" roared Billy in a rage so fearsome, even Malky recognised backing down as his only sensible option.

Shaking his head, regaining his feet, Malky held out his hands in submission.

"Sorry, Billy, that was out of order, I didn't mean anything by it. Just the drink talking. Let's call it a night and we can deal wi' the lassies the morra, eh."

"Aye, whatever, fuck off out of my sight before I batter your cunt in. I've got things to do."

The two men went their separate ways.

Despite the calendar confirming this as a Spring night, the damp air made it feel frigid. Malky stumbled and weaved toward his flat, alcohol numbing him to any sense of unseasonal chill. Automatic pilot. A journey made so often it could be accomplished without need for conscious thought.

Andris Balodis followed about twenty yards behind. Malky's obvious drunkenness didn't negate caution. He kept checking behind, making sure Billy didn't return and attempt a reconciliation. Andris witnessed the brother's violent disagreement from across the street, melting into the shadows of an alleyway to avoid being noticed. Their conflict gave him the desired separation he knew he'd need in order to make a (literal) fist of revenge.

Malky took out his keys, eventually finding the lock and pushing open his front door. Andris ran, closing the gap between them in an instant. Malky turned when he heard the footsteps. Everything went black.

15. WHO NEEDS ENEMIES?

Cammy could hear the blood whooshing in his ears as the sky above him spun, dazzling lights circling with his pain. The punch came out of nowhere. One minute he was standing puffing on his ciggie, the next, flat on his back.

The swirling, swimming features of Bart replaced the dancing lights. His voice sounded hollow, like speaking from far off, even though his rancid breath indicated close proximity.

"I fuckin knew you were holding out on me you wank. I spoke to Tina this morning and she told me your Ma won millions on the lottery. So, where's our share you greedy wee fuck?"

Cammy's jaw throbbed, he struggled to clear the fog in his head, struggled to form a coherent answer.

"Stop mumbling you wee dick and get up. Fuck's sake, I hardly touched you."

Badger shuffled uncomfortably in the background. Hardly touched him? He'd seen cricket bats deployed with less force than Bart's right hook. Badger was torn, really wanted to help his pal, but that psycho Simpson would likely batter him as well if he showed any sympathy or support.

Cammy rolled onto his side and attempted to push himself up. Just as he seemed to be making progress toward standing, the boot went into his ribs and he collapsed onto his front, gasping, tears and snot flowing reflexively from the shock of the impact.

Bart sat down on his haunches and pulled Cammy's head up by his hair, whispering coldly into his ear.

"You listen to me carefully, McDuff. I want money. Lots of money...or else. Do you understand what I'm saying?"

Cammy understood the implications, knew Simpson meant it. He'd play along, for the moment. But, if the cunt imagined Cammy meekly handing over a pile of notes, he'd misjudged the situation badly. Bart was going to regret this. When you lived amongst people with little to look forward to and nothing to lose, money could buy you some very unsavoury favours. None of his new found fortune would be finding its way into the pockets or bank account of Bart, Cammy was absolutely sure about that.

"Ok Bart, I'll sort you out some money."

Simpson let go of his hair and stood.

"Right Badger, let's get to fuck. Richard Branson here is off to buy us some booze. Good stuff mind, bottles of voddy, cans of decent lager, none of that pishy cider. Aren't you, McDuff?"

The nodded assent was painful and grudged. Badger tried to convey his apologies with his eyes. Cammy saw it and understood. If their places had been reversed, he wouldn't have intervened either. The revelation that he was the son of a millionaire after all, helped soothe his aches and pains.

Ok, Mr Tarantino, get ready to peek through your fingers and feel like you're going to spew.

Cammy got back to the house following the run-in with Simpson to find his parents absent, as usual. Opening the fridge revealed even paltrier rations than normal. According to Billy, Stella disappeared on Sunday. Since then, his feckless father failed miserably to undertake any domestic duties – buying food included. Cammy's stomach growled like a pissed off dog but there really was nothing worth eating, little that looked fit for consumption in fact. Slamming the door shut in disgust, it soon became apparent pickings from the kitchen cupboards were equally slim. Sometimes his parents' inability to provide the basics in life made him furious. They were hopeless, always had been.

Stella's absconding seemed like the biggest boot in the scrotum she could deliver him; all of them. Of course, he and she bickered constantly, she voiced disapproval with almost every aspect of his life, and he was often less than cooperative, but this was beyond the pale. Running off with all that money, leaving him to face Simpson, leaving him and Jack in the woefully inadequate hands of their too-often-drunk-for-his-own-good father.

Cammy climbed the stairs and pulled out the bottom drawer of the chest opposite his bed. Retrieving the small plastic bag taped to the frame, he took out the last twenty. Enough to get a carry-out and a fish supper. He replaced the remaining few quid and pushed the drawer back into its slot. This was the only hiding place to so far elude all his thieving bastard family members and he was very careful about when he accessed it.

Just short of twenty quid's worth of booze might be enough to appease Simpson until he got his hands on some serious dough, Lottery dough. He knew exactly where his mother would be; in London with his shirtlifting older brother. If he had to, he'd get on a train, go down there and force the miserable bitch to stump up.

Something made Cammy stop at the foot of the stairs, just as he was about to leave for the off licence and chippy. All this time, he watched and endured as his thieving relatives helped themselves to his things, his money. There was nobody in, which was a rare occurrence; somebody could usually be relied upon to be glued to the television in any given hour on any given day. How was his father able to afford the pub but couldn't provide a pint of milk or a slice of toast? He must have a stash, some money hidden away like Cammy did. It was time to find it.

Room by room Cammy rifled through drawers, lifted up clothes and pulled back furniture. Finally, in the kitchen, on top of a unit, in a biscuit barrel they no longer used, he found it. He nearly fell off the stool he was standing on. A thick roll of notes expanded to virtually fill the entire inside of the tin. Where the fuck had his dad got this kind of money from? The miserable shit was out getting pissed up, while Cammy took a pounding from the local hard man, with his stomach touching his backbone in hunger. He stepped down and pulled the cash free from its container. After staring at it in disbelief for a few seconds, he sorted the notes into separate piles of tens and twenties. Three grand. Three, fucking, grand. Three thousand and sixty pounds to be exact. Was this enough to have Simpson rubbed out? Dealt with maybe, scared off, probably not buried. Then again, if he stole this money from his dad, it wasn't Simpson who'd soon be wearing a wooden overcoat, it would be Cammy. One thing he did know, his dad's mathematical abilities were limited, taking some of this wad should be ok. He decided on keeping the total above three thousand. Going below that milestone figure may just be significant enough to alert even his numerically challenged father.

Cammy removed fifty pounds and put the rest back. Seventy quid. Flush for the first time in ages. As well as booze, he'd be able to score some weed, maybe even a wrap of speed. This would buy time. Get Simpson's hopes up, make him think Cammy had capitulated to his bullying. That way, when he got hold of the cash he needed, revenge would taste all the sweeter. Cammy smiled to himself. He knew exactly how to get the money.

***

Greg Marshall trembled, anger threatening to overwhelm him. The words stared back from the page; scrawled, barely legible but entirely clear in their meaning and intent.

What drove a father to say such hideous things about a sick child? Greg understood the McDuffs may have received some bogus letters but his was so obviously genuine. Resentment snaked through his capillaries. The injustice of scum like them getting their paws on an unwarranted, unearned fortune while his poor, sweet boy was condemned by lack of funds to die in agony before his life even got going. It couldn't be right. It wasn't right.

He wouldn't take this from these animals. Brandon deserved more respect. Greg deserved more respect goddammit. Since his wife died in childbirth, Greg's every waking moment and most of his dreams were devoted to raising his son, caring for him, nursing him, soothing him. This was not happening. He would not be treated like this by anyone.

Greg wasn't interested in the McDuff's reputation, he'd be fighting back. It was just plain wrong. Sitting on a mountain of money, unwilling to help Brandon; an innocent. Well, they didn't know it yet but they'd be coughing up, and Brandon would be going to America for treatment.

16. AMOEBA

"Shut it!"

The voice hissed like water hitting hot fat and the gag tightened, rendering further protest impossible. Tears dampened the blindfold but his captor took no heed, showed no mercy, no sympathy.

"I warned you about making a noise and I meant it. You're going to lie there, keep quiet and do as you're told." A jabbing finger pressed into his chest.

The car started to move. Exhaust fumes clawed harshly at his throat; engine and road noise exaggerated by the dulling of other senses. The floor of the car's boot cold, hard and made all the more uncomfortable by the ropes binding hands behind back and ankles together. He felt smaller than usual, like a sheet of silver foil that's been rolled into a tight ball, more vulnerable than ever before. Not scared: petrified.

Minutes passed uncounted with neither watch nor experience to rely on to judge their number. Each time the car slowed, his heart rate increased proportionately; anticipating the return of his tormentor, the reaching of their unnamed destination, and whatever fate that might bring. When the motor finally quietened, and he heard the door open and close again, the certainty was almost a relief.

Lifted roughly from the boot, he found himself slung over a shoulder. Defiance flooded into him in a crashing

109

wave and, despite the restrictions of the gag, he bit as forcefully as possible into the nearest scapular.

"Oh, you wee...!"

Concrete introduced itself with enthusiasm; pain surged through his arms and back. With the wind knocked from his lungs, he gasped for oxygen, panicking as his heaving chest failed to locate any. The slap around the face chased off the last lingering trace of boldness. When air finally rushed back, tears and compliance kept it company.

"Don't try anything like that again or you'll be sorry! Right?"

Re-slung and whimpering in self pity, they descended. Jangling of keys, fumbling with handles and locks, set down on a mattress. The ropes untied and the blindfold removed. A bright light shone in his eyes, dazzling and disorientating, obscuring, preventing recognition.

"Ok, here's how it is, wee man. You're staying here for as long as it takes to get my money. If you don't give me any grief, I won't give you any. Don't bother shouting coz no-one will hear you. There's juice and biscuits and a games console. I'll be back to give you food every now and again. If you need to go, use the bucket."

The dazzling light backed off. The overhead bulb flicked on - just a glimpse, nothing tangible, a balaclava. There was something about the voice. The door closed, locked and bolted.

The room was small, a single window; boarded up, metal grille fixed over it. The mattress he'd been dumped on lay bedless on the floor. A duvet and pillow set featuring Scooby Doo added a splash of colour. As promised, a tray with a glass of orange cordial and a couple of chocolate biscuits also adorned the dull-coloured carpet. In different circumstances, the Nintendo DS might prove alluring but, here, offered scant consolation. The bucket his only other companion.

A single cell organism.

He hugged his knees, rocked gently back and forth, and

wondered where his Mum was.

17. OH BROTHER, WHERE ART THOU?

Stark stood at the grave, hands in pockets, mind idling. A whole week had passed since he started the new job. It had flown in.

Tom Stark, father and husband. A guid man.
Carrie Stark, sister and daughter. Taken too soon.

Loss featured prominently in most folks lives and those who'd reached their thirties would be doing well not to have experienced it. His mourning came with a side order of guilt. Stark stood there turning back time, doing things differently, saving Carrie from her boyfriend, from herself. The fact they were twins really did make a difference, one in the same, two of a kind, a single egg split in two in the womb, now divided for ever.

Once again, he felt the dark shadow of the reaper as it crept across his last remaining loved one. Mary was ill, he could tell she was holding something back, something bad. He was a trained detective, but it wouldn't have taken Sherlock Holmes' powers of deduction to work that one out.

The Ochil Hills loomed, dramatic and beautiful. Not directly above the cemetery but close enough to impart a sense of grandeur to the setting. He looked over at the craggy face of Craigleith and drifted into thoughts about the fragile, fleeting nature of human life compared to the solid, permanence of such geological features. In reality, even these monoliths were on borrowed time. One day, in the far distant future, they'd succumb to the elements, be no more.

A cool wind curled round the headstones, Stark shivered, suppressing tears and panic. The ringing phone jarred him back into the here and now.

"Stark speaking."

"Hi, sir, it's Ian. Are you on your way in?"

"Aye, just stopped off for a minute to do something. What's up?"

"Been a bit of a development wi' the McDuffs. Seems like Jack, the youngest of Billy's laddies, has gone missing now."

"Oh, for fuck's sake. Are they sure this time? He's no' round at Tina's pals' house is he?"

"Naw, apparently not. Billy's freaking out. Claiming that Graham Connelly must have taken him, eh."

"Of course, who else would it be. Right, I'll see you in about five minutes. Cheers."

"Ok sir, cheers."

The briefing room was less rowdy than normal. Stark thought the unwelcome guest from up the road might be the cause of the reserved tone of proceedings. Unsurprisingly, DI McGhee was back, trying to reassert his seniority and experience in such matters and no doubt belittle Stark in the process. They got a standard introduction from DCI McLaren regarding the case and McGhee's involvement before he handed over to the paunchy, arrogant looking prick.

"Thanks, sir. As far as we can tell, Jack McDuff, went missing after fitba practice yesterday evening. The father, Billy, got home late from the pub and only noticed the laddie was missing this morning when he went to get him ready for school. He checked with the fitba coach, who confirmed the boy left on time as usual. He tried the auntie and a next door neighbour but when neither had seen Jack, he called us.

"It's fair to say, he's not too keen on cooperating with the police. However, Jack's only nine and even someone as staunchly anti-polis as Billy McDuff knows he needs our help right now."

"Where's the mother, sir? Could he be with her?" asked one of the Stirling team McGhee brought with him.

"No, apparently, these lovely, upstanding citizens have won the lottery and the mother appears to have buggered off somewhere with the winnings."

A rumble of surprise and confirmation moved through the assemblage.

"Social Services are well aware of the family and, as you know, the boy's cousin, Tina, recently performed her own disappearing act. However, as I said, Jack McDuff's only nine and the chances of him being with some pals is much less likely. We have to bear in mind that his parents have won a fortune, kidnap and blackmail are distinct possibilities."

Annoyingly, Stark couldn't help thinking McGhee was actually turning out to be a good cop, a smooth operator, confident, assured. He so wanted him to be a tosser.

"I've put a map up showing the fitba pitches and the McDuff house. I've also marked on what would be the laddie's normal route back from one to the other. You'll split into teams, conduct the door-to-door. I'm going to interview Billy McDuff, his brother Malky, and the auntie – Maureen. Oh, and the fitba coach. He's a Latvian guy called Edgars Balodis. Been here for years.

"A dog team will search the laddie's route home initially and then we'll fan out from there if they draw a blank. Any questions?"

With none forthcoming the DCI wrapped things up, taking on the role of liaison with the media and re-iterating, it felt almost entirely for Stark's benefit, that DI McGhee had operational control.

***

115

Billy couldn't get his head around this at all. Why weren't the cops out finding that pervert Connelly? He should have been their first port of call, the obvious choice. The dirty bastard better hope Billy didn't get to him before the police, or a house fire would slip well down the rankings of unpleasant things that happened to him in recent years.

The other thing bothering Billy was where Malky had gotten to. Not answering his phone or his door, and no word since they parted on less than amicable terms three evenings previous. Normally, they would meet back in the pub, make it up over a beer, but not this time. Jonny Jacobs had been a bit off with him, likely thanks to Malky's over-the-top attack on the two young guys on his premises. The landlord seemed under pressure, struggling with money; probably the last thing he needed was a load of hassle from the cops. Billy would be upset if the pub shut. Maybe he could buy Jonny out if Stella ever stumped up his share of the lottery money? Being a publican sounded like a fuckin brilliant idea.

Malky had always been a moody wee shite, but this extended huff was odd, especially as he knew Billy had a forgiving nature when it came to his brother's petulance. Christ, there'd been more than a few previous instances. They'd made plans, had things to do. More importantly, Billy had dosh. Lots of it, and a route to getting a whole lot more.

Billy held the mobile phone, staring at the screen; Stella's number glared back at him. She was a bitch, a thieving bitch; but still his wife, still Jack's mum, and as such, deserved to know. On the other hand, she was a bitch, a thieving bitch, who didn't deserve to be called Jack's mother and he'd gladly kill her with his bare hands if he could get a hold of her.

Mo the mouth. She could pass on the message.

"Mo?"

"Aye. What is it, Billy? I hope you're no' going to start about that money an' Stella because I don't know where she is, eh."

"Shut the fuck up, Mo. Just letting you know that Jack's gone missing."

"What?"

"Went to get him ready for school an' there was no sign of him."

"Jesus Christ! Have you been to the polis?"

"Aye, for all the fuckin good it's done me. You can tell Stella."

Billy cancelled the call before Mo could say anything else. She immediately rang back but he let it go to voicemail. He couldn't be arsed dealing with her. Malky's phone remained switched off according to the message he got. Billy shoved on his trainers without untying them. If the police weren't going to find Jack, he bloody well was. First off, the pub, take the edge off his nerves, give him time to think. Thinking time would be important, allow him to come up with a plan of action.

***

Juris looked at his father, face pale and drawn with worry and a lack of sleep.

"Hi, Tētis."

Edgars was sinking into the warm water of semi-consciousness when his son's croaked greeting brought him bursting to the surface, gasping for air.

"Juris! You're awake. How are you, son?"

"I'm ok. What happened?"

"You were attacked and hurt badly. We are waiting for you to wake up. Praying. Now God has answered us."

Juris had no recollection of anything much. A vague memory of meeting Pete to go for a pint but that was all. His body ached and throbbed.

"Where's Svece?"

"She's at home. She's exhausted. We are taking turns to be sitting here with you."

"Andy?"

"Not sure. We go back and forward from here a lot and every day he is going to college, I don't know. He was here on night it happened and day after. I think not yesterday but day before too."

"Pete? Was he with me? Is he ok?"

"Yes, Pete is good. He's not hurt as bad as you. The doctor send him home. What happened, son? Who did this to you?"

"I don't know, Dad. I don't really remember anything. I met Pete and we said we'd go for a drink. That's it. Nothing else."

Even this short conversation knocked the stuffing out of Juris. He felt his eyes droop and his father noticed it too.

"It is ok, son. You rest. I go tell your mother you are awake. I see you later."

Juris drifted off, thoughts of his brother coming to the fore and an uneasiness he couldn't quite work out the basis of.

***

"It's really unlike him, Ian. He's never late for our appointments and always puts the kettle on. Seems glad of some adult company, eh."

"Aye, well, I can understand that. Must be really hard bringing up that laddie on his own, especially wi' all the problems the wee man has. I'm sure he's fine. Just got a lot on an' forgot."

"Aye, no doubt. Anyway, I'll see you later on. Love you."

"Aye, me too."

Barr put his phone back in his pocket and shrugged partly in apology and partly in embarrassment. Stark wasn't even looking.

The two cops were standing in the street having

completed their third door-to-door, with little to show for it. People wanted to help find the kid but just hadn't seen anything.

"I'm no' convinced this is going to get us anywhere, sir."

"No, me neither, but sometimes it works. It's just a bit frustrating. The first few hours of these things are the critical ones."

Stark's phone vibrated in his pocket and he fished it out. The number was unrecognised. He braced himself for some automated crap from a firm of ambulance chasers or those bloody PPI folk.

"DI Stark?"

"Aye."

"This is Jim McGhee here. I was hoping you might fancy helping me out with some of the familial interviews? Someone told me you know them and having just checked out your CV, letting you tramp the streets with the uniforms and DCs seems like a bit of a waste of your talents."

Stark was taken aback, convinced McGhee would feel the same way about him as McLaren, take great delight in belittling him. He'd clearly done the man a disservice.

"Ok, aye. I'd love to help out if you want me to."

"Right, good. Can you get back to the station as soon as please, I've got a couple of folk out picking up Billy McDuff. We'll start with him."

"No bother. I'll be with you in a few minutes. Cheers."

Barr stood with his hands on his hips and sighed. "Is that you getting to do the good stuff then sir, while I carry on wi' the trawling?"

"Afraid so, Ian. I'll need to take the car. I'll send someone else out to give you a hand though."

"You're all heart, sir."

Stark grinned and walked away, feeling a lot better about life than he had done earlier in the day.

18. ROOM WITHOUT A VIEW

Jack pulled at the door with all his strength but it wouldn't budge. Multiple attempts failed. The mesh around the window no more cooperative – digging into the flesh of his small fingers, taunting him by remaining firmly in place. Shouting, banging and any manner of other noises went unheeded; just as his kidnapper predicted. A fit of petulance resulted in the games console being reduced to its component parts; an action he now deeply regretted. His was a short attention span at the best of times but this level of boredom was way beyond anything he'd ever endured before. The meagre rations went by the wayside early on and he was hungry.

None of those things mattered compared to the bucket. Holding on as long as he could, eventually he relented. It was likely a cruel, practical joke, played on him by his own twisted mind that he ended up defecating rather than just peeing. At the moment of release it felt novel, rebellious even, but that notion was soon sent packing. It reeked. Really, really stank and there was no relief from it. Every time he thought he'd gotten used to it and the stench was not so bad, he made the mistake of moving across the room or standing up, or sitting down. Whenever he did, the foul aroma would return with shitty, stinking vengeance.

He felt sorry for himself, confused, disorientated. Nothing made sense. What was his abductor going on about? Money? His family were broke. As poor as any other he knew, poorer than most. Somebody at the football asked about them winning the lottery but it couldn't be true because his parents hadn't mentioned anything. Something that big would've caused a celebration, a ceremony or something. Did this nutcase believe the rumour, think he could get some of this fictitious money? He worried even more because he really didn't think his parents had the money for a ransom, and if they didn't...

The rattle of the key in the lock made him start. A wave of panic followed this adrenalin rush. His kidnapper was back. No telling what might happen now. Jack had to do something, try to escape, get help. He looked for something he could use to narrow the physical mismatch between them. Nothing.

Well, there was one thing.

The door opened and the man reached in and switched off the light, shining the dazzling beam of the torch in Jack's eyes again. It was now or never, he needed the element of surprise for this to work. He ran forward and flung the contents of the bucket out toward the bright light.

"Eat my shit you motherfucker!"

This outburst made Jack feel powerful, in control, like he had a chance. This would work. He was out of here.

"Jesus Christ, you dirty, manky wee bastard!"

The torch fell to the floor and Jack made for the door. The kidnapper spluttered and coughed, emitting a constant stream of language almost as foul as Jack's evacuations as he tried to squeeze past him. Hands grabbed but Jack twisted, wriggled and fought. Breaking free, he ran. The stairwell was poorly lit and he failed to judge the last step carefully enough. Tumbling and rolling he came to a thudding stop back at the foot of the staircase. He tried to stand but the kidnapper was on him.

"You stupid, dirty wee fucker! You're really going to

regret that decision, wee man. Really regret it."

Jack was hauled to his feet and dragged kicking and screaming back into the room where he was trussed hand and foot, blindfolded and dumped back on the mattress.

He could hear the laboured breathing of his assailant, rising and falling in tandem with his own thudding heartbeat. Aches and a stinging sensation from his knee began to creep over him now the adrenalin was subsiding. The guy took a few moments to compose himself, spitting and swearing relentlessly as he did so.

"That was a very fuckin stupid thing to do, wee man, eh. I told you we'd be fine if you did as you were told, but naw, you thought you'd be clever, try something daft. Well, there's no way I'm having you chuck a bucket of shite over me again, so here's how it's going to be from now on.

"You're going to stay tied up tonight. You'll get one bite to eat a day, maybe. When you need to shite or piss, you can wait until I get here an' supervise you. If you can't wait, do it in your drawers. If I get paid soon, you'll no' have to put up wi' it for that long. Then again, if I don't get paid quick, it could get pretty messy for you."

"Why are you doing this to me? My Ma and Da's no' got any money."

"Aye right, son. We both know they won the lottery and now they're rich. Well, I don't think that's fair. I want a share, an' you're going to help me get it."

"They haven't won the lottery, that's just a rumour. We're skint. You'll no' get any money."

"Good try, wee man, but we both know you're bluffing."

"I'm no' bluffing they don't have any money. Please let me go, please."

Jack started to thrash about on the mattress in desperation and frustration. The kidnapper grabbed him forcefully by the shoulders, pinning him until he stilled.

"Listen to me, wee man. This is your last warning. You better behave yourself. Stay quiet, do as I tell you and everything will be just fine an' dandy. If you fuck me about again, there won't be any more food, and these ropes will stay on full time. Do you understand?"

Jack nodded slightly.

"Sorry, I don't think I heard that."

"Aye, ok, I understand. Please don't hurt me, mister."

The door thumped shut, the key rattled in the lock again. The smell returned to torment him but so did that voice.

19. LET'S TALK

Stark shook McGhee's hand.

"Thanks for bringing me into the fold. Appreciate it."

"No bother, Adam. Between you and me, Crockett's a bit of a wanker. He wouldn't know a good polis if he came up and knocked the hat off his head. Too busy playing politics an' worrying about promotion to make the right call."

Stark couldn't help but grin.

"Well, it's fair to say he hasn't exactly welcomed me wi' open arms. One of them things. It's my own fault for leaving the big city lights behind. Was always going to leave me up against it wi' certain types."

"Aye, well, I couldn't give a shit about that. You've got the experience and training we need to get this thing sorted quickly, so let's get on wi' it. I'm off to see if they've picked up Billy McDuff yet – wasn't at home apparently. You any ideas for likely hang outs?"

"If old form is anything to go by, I'd be inclined towards the pub. I think the Cross Words is our best bet."

"Funny name for a pub?"

"Oh, sorry, that's a local joke about all the fights that go on there. It's the Cross Swords, down in the town centre. It was always the favoured watering hole of Billy an' his mates."

"You know this guy from back in the day then?"

"Aye, we were at school together. Long time ago now

125

mind. He might be a changed man. I doubt it, but you never know."

"Nah, I'll go with your instinct. Leopards like McDuff rarely change their spots. I'll send a couple of the CHIMPS over there."

Stark smiled as McGhee walked off. The government introduced Community Support Officers in England as a money-saving device; a way of augmenting the police force with cheap bodies, purportedly improving community relations, increasing visibility and hence reassurance for those who believed beat bobbies deterred crime. They had limited powers of arrest and far less training than the real police force. This caused deep resentment and concern amongst the rank and file officers. Rather unkindly, but also understandably, the nickname CHIMPS arose – Completely Hopeless In Most Policing Situations. In Scotland, the equivalent was the Community Warden, allegedly more effective and without any powers of arrest but they didn't escape the brickbats or banter because of it.

From the other side of the glass, Billy, freshly plucked from his perch at the Cross Swords bar, looked sullen, uncooperative. Stark knew this was not going to be an enjoyable experience. McGhee came into the ante room to give him the nod.

"Ready?"

"Aye, let's go an' see what Billy boy has to say for himself."

Billy smelt as unkempt as he looked. It may have been the stress and trauma at misplacing his youngest child but Stark thought it unlikely, reckoned this probably constituted business as usual for Billy. The cloying, stick in the back of your throat aroma of days' worth of sweat, was genuinely unpleasant in this enclosed space.

As soon as he clocked Stark, his hackles rose.

"Oh, fuckin brilliant, Adam Stark. What the fuck am I doing in here and why the fuck are you lot no' out there trying to get my laddie back?"

McGhee took control straight away as the two policemen took their seats opposite Billy. An old stager, well used to putting the likes of McDuff in his place with a polite, professional, take no shit approach.

"Good afternoon to you too, Billy. I'm Detective Inspector Jim McGhee and, as you know, this is Detective Inspector Adam Stark. You'll be pleased to hear we're throwing as much resource as we can at this enquiry and we're very hopeful of finding Jack quickly. However, we need to speak to as many people as possible to try and help us do that. As his Dad, and the one who reported him missing, you top our list. Ok?"

Billy merely shrugged and shook his head, folded his arms and looked to the corner of the room in apparent boredom. He did sullen schoolchild far better than his nine year old could ever have.

"When did you first notice Jack was missing?"

"When I got up to get him ready for school, eh."

"What time was that?"

"About eight."

"And when did you last see him?"

"No' sure, probably when he went off to fitba practice the night before."

Stark and McGhee both scribbled notes as they talked.

"What about after fitba practice? Were you no' at home when he was due back?" asked Stark.

Billy shifted in his seat, leaning forward, right fist clenched inside the palm of his left hand, taking Stark's eye directly as he replied. "Naw, I was out. How? Is that a crime now is it?"

"Well, technically, it could be, Billy. Jack's only nine. He shouldn't be coming home to an empty house."

"It wasn't an empty house. His brother was in to look after him, right!" He banged his fist down hard as he spoke.

McGhee cut in, "Look, Billy, let's no' get all defensive

and aggressive here. We're trying to find a wee boy who's gone missing. Just answer the questions an' it'll help us get him back quicker. We're all on the same side here."

"Aye, right! Are we fuck! You lot are just fuckin itching to get me on something instead of finding that dirty, bastard pervert Connelly and stopping him from interfering wi' my laddie!"

McGhee sighed deeply. "Billy, I understand you're worried and stressed about all this but if you won't help us, you're no' helping Jack. Right?"

Billy returned to defensive, closed postures.

"I asked if you understood me, Billy. Do you?"

Again the dismissive shrug and sneer.

"You said your older boy, Cameron, was in the house. If we speak to him, he'll confirm that will he?" McGhee continued.

"Aye, of course."

"What about his mother? Are you two no' living together any more?"

Again, Billy reacted angrily, sitting forward with fists clenched, a fire burning in his eyes. "She's done a runner. I've no fuckin idea where she is, before you ask. Taken my money an' fucked off, the thieving cow!"

"Sorry, what do you mean taken your money? Are you saying she's robbed you, Billy? Do you want to file a complaint?" asked Stark.

"Don't try an' rip the piss out of me, you. You already know - everybody knows. We won the lottery an' she took all the money an' fucked off wi' it somewhere. If you want to find out where, ask that scheming cow of a sister of hers."

"Won the lottery? Jeezo, congratulations. How much?" asked McGhee.

"No idea. Millions apparently."

"Well, we'll certainly need to talk to Maureen, ask her if she knows where Stella has gone. We'd like to talk to Stella as well, for obvious reasons. I take it she's aware her son is missing?"

"Well, I told Mo to tell her, so she should know by now, aye."

McGhee paused for a moment, reading over his notes, letting Billy settle. Stark liked him a lot.

"Right, so, getting back to last night. Where were you when Jack was at practice?"

"Up the Cross Swords."

"And I assume the barman or landlord can verify that?"

"Aye, of course."

"So, you get home, don't check on the boy, and go to bed when?"

"Jesus, I just thought he'd be in bed. I was a bit pissed, right. I've no idea when I went to bed. Probably about midnight, eh."

"And you reported Jack missing this morning?"

"Aye. At about eight thirty. Once I'd checked wi' his brother, Auntie Mo an' a few pals in case they knew where he was."

"Right. What about since then? Our boys picked you up in the pub. Seems a strange thing to do when your son's gone missing – to go for a drink?"

"Oh aye, here we go again. Having a go at me. On the same side - my hairy ring piece we are! You two are implying something aren't you, eh? You think I've got something to do wi' this?"

"Look, Billy, we've been over this. We need to ask you stuff, you need to answer calmly and honestly. The more fuss you make, the more likely we are to start thinking maybe you have got something to do with Jack's disappearance. Why were you in the pub?"

"I was trying to think, get my head together, steady my nerves. It's no' every day your laddie gets kidnapped by a paedo. I wanted to try an' work out where that manky bastard might have taken him an' then go an' get him back."

Again, McGhee paused, altering a few notes, letting Billy's flush of anger subside slightly.

"Billy, you said everybody knows you won the lottery. Have you thought about that for a minute?"

"What do you mean, likes?"

"Well, that's a lot of money. Very tempting. Somebody might fancy a share?"

"Aye, well good fuckin luck to them. Nobody fucks wi' the McDuffs and gets away wi' it!"

The look Billy fired towards Stark filled the space between them in the room and the intervening years since their own altercation. They both knew this was a threat aimed at Stark as well as anyone who might want to steal or extort money from Billy.

"That's as maybe, Billy," continued McGhee, "but that kind of cash can make desperate folk do desperate things. Have you checked your mail this morning?"

"Naw. It'll just be loads of begging letters an' bills, eh."

"Probably, but we need to be sure this isn't a kidnap for a ransom. No unusual texts or voicemails?"

Billy took out his phone and scrolled through the screen.

"Nothing obvious."

"Please check your mail when you get home, make sure there's nothing there."

"Aye, but it'll be a waste of fuckin time. Bills and beggars, that's all it'll be."

"Ok, we'll leave it there for now, Billy. Oh, no, sorry, one more thing. What about Malky, your brother? Did you no' contact him about Jack? You didn't mention him earlier."

"I've no' heard from Malky for a few days."

Stark cut in, "I thought you two were tight? What's happened? Had a fall out?"

"No' that it's any of your business, but we did have a bit of a ruck the other day. It's fuck all, happens all the time. He'll sulk for a while, then just turn up like nothing happened."

"Is he jealous of the money?"

"Is he fuck. He knows I'll see him right. If I ever get my share from that thieving bitch of a wife that is."

McGhee decided to stop things there. They'd pushed enough buttons for now. It was going to be a long day and it was important to keep some of their powder dry for later.

"Ok, we'll have a wee chat wi' Malky as well in due course but off you go the now, Billy. Get back to us if you find anything suspicious in the mail. Alright?"

Billy pushed his chair back forcefully and stormed out of the room without saying anything more, his sudden movement trailing his foetid odour across the cops' nostrils with renewed vigour.

"Fuck me, he could do wi' a good bath!"

Coughing, McGhee nodded his assent.

"So, what do you think, Jim?"

The older man ran his pen up and down his notes, tapping it occasionally as he went.

"Difficult to tell. As you know only too well, most child abductions and murders are carried out by family members. I'm no' sure he's the type, as uncouth as he is. Need to keep an open mind though, an' get on wi' interviewing the rest of the clan. You?"

"Aye, much the same. Something's no' right but I can't quite work out what. The Connelly thing seems like a distraction tactic to me. He keeps hammering it too forcefully, too convinced that's the only option."

"Yeah, maybe, but this isn't an educated and reasonable guy we're talking about here. Scapegoats and lazy logic are just as likely, but I hear what you're saying. It's a possibility he's trying to lead us away from looking closer to home."

Commotion and raised voices interrupted their musing. They both walked quickly toward the reception area to see what was going on.

"You fuckin bitch, where's the money? Where's my

fuckin money?"

"Fuck you, it's my money, and where's my son?"

Stella McDuff was sitting on a chair, a reddish welt on her left cheek, blood dripping from her nose. Maureen was comforting her, while a female officer stood between them and the thrashing ball of testosterone that was Billy McDuff and three cops trying to restrain him, one of them Ian Barr.

Stark strode forward. "Billy, calm down or I'm going to spray you, do you hear me, Billy?"

"Fuck you! That thieving, lying cow stole my money. Arrest her why don't you?"

"Billy, this is your last warning, calm down and stop shouting and swearing or I'm going to pepper spray you."

"Fuck you, pig!"

"Right lads let him go and stand back."

Billy leapt up, only to meet the full force of the pepper spray jet connecting with his face. The effect was instantaneous. Choking, coughing, and spitting, he dropped to his knees and then all fours. His breath wheezed and hacked out of him as he struggled to cope with the fire engulfing his head. Ian Barr handcuffed him and, with the help of a colleague, dragged him off to the cells.

"Fuck you Billy, you bastard. You're going down for this for definite."

"Maureen, that's enough. We'll deal wi' Billy. If you can't keep your language civil in here I'll have to arrest you as well,"said Stark.

"What? Arrest me? Look at her, eh! Look what that animal did to my sister!"

"Maureen, I can see, but you're not helping."

Stark turned to the female officer. "Can you get Stella some first aid please and take her to an interview room once we know she's ok? Thanks.

"Maureen, go outside, have a cigarette and calm down. We need to talk to you as well but not when you're behaving like this."

"Fuck's sake. You lot are a joke! My nephew's missing, my sister's been assaulted an' you're telling me to calm down!"

Stark stood closer to the irate woman. "Maureen, you can go out and get some air and a smoke or you can go into a cell. What's it to be?"

She stomped out the door, already smoking by the time it closed behind her. She stared furiously back through the glass at Stark, who turned away.

"Well done Adam, mate. Nicely handled."

"Aye, it's no' the first time I've had to deal wi' the likes of the McDuffs, Jim."

"Well, despite the furore, it's actually saved us a bit of time and effort trying to track down the wife. Let's go and get cleaned up, have a cup of tea and get ready to speak to the women. See what they've got to say for themselves."

"Actually, Jim, I've just thought. There's probably nobody at the McDuff house the now is there? I mean, if the wee man does turn up like his cousin did, we'll no' realise. I reckon we need to post a car outside. Also means if the older laddie is there we can get him brought in to check Billy's story out as well. What do you think?"

"Good point, Adam. I'll get the CHIMPS on it. Even they couldn't fuck up sitting in a car for a few hours." McGhee winked and walked away.

***

"Pete, it's Juris, how's it going?"

"Juris! I'm fine thanks mate, glad to hear you're back in the land of the living again."

"Aye, head's still ringing and the stookie on my arm is as itchy as fuck but I'm a lot better.

"Pete, what the fuck happened the other night?"

His friend sighed deeply.

"We should never have gone in the Cross Words, mate.

That was my fault. I should have known we'd get into bother, eh."

"Aye, we never go in there, what the fuck were we thinking about?"

"I've got no idea, mate. I'm really sorry."

"Look, Pete, don't blame yourself. It wasn't you that battered fuck out of us both. Who was it by the way? Do you know?"

Again, a long pause and a sigh. "Aye, as soon as I saw him, I should have got us the fuck out of there but you were at the bar too quick. It was Malky McDuff. He lamped me first, I blacked out an' then he went after you, eh."

"Fuck, if I'd known that mental case was in there I'd have given it a wide berth."

"Aye, me an' all. Sorry man."

"Pete, for fuck's sake, it wasn't your fault."

Another short silence ensued.

"Listen, Pete, have you seen or heard from Andris in the last couple of days? He's no' been up to the hospital an' my folks are getting a bit worried about him."

"Aw, shit."

"What? What's the score, Pete, what's going on?"

"It's probably nothing but Andy made me tell him who fucked you up an' he got pretty wound up about it. Said he was going to sort McDuff out."

"Sort McDuff out! What the fuck?"

"I know, I know. I told him to stay away from him, the guy's a radge bastard, an' to just let it go, but he was pure raging."

"Aw, man, that's not good. Andy's a nightmare when he loses his temper. Aw, fuck. I hope he's no' actually done something stupid."

"I don't know, mate. I hope no' either, eh."

"Alright, Pete, I need to go. Let me know if you see Andy, an' if you do, tell him to get up here an' bring me some fuckin grapes!"

They laughed, the quip breaking the tension that had been twisting between them like a viper in the last few moments of their conversation. However, once the phone was back under his pillow, Juris couldn't help but feel anxious.

20. CHIMPS TEA PARTY

Michael Turner enjoyed being a Community Warden. He'd always wanted to join the police, but he failed the entrance exams. After a couple of dead end jobs, he spent a year unemployed before landing the Warden's job. This was all the fun of the fair without any of the real responsibility. The money was pretty shit but, as a way of filling his day, it eclipsed sitting in the house while his retired Dad carped on about him being a lazy, waste of space. The biggest bonus of all, his partner, Debbie Lynch. Smoking hot at the best of times but in that uniform? He struggled all day to control his semi.

They were sitting in the car outside the McDuff house. Sent out to do the usual low-level, menial job that there just weren't enough real police to allocate to any more. He didn't really mind. It meant lots of time in close proximity to the delicious Debbie.

Debbie Lynch decided her time as a Community Warden would lead to a proper police job. She knew the difference. Her Dad was a cop, her grandpa had been a cop. She would be a cop one day too. All the budget cuts and a slight weight problem had limited her chances of getting past the application stage, but she'd stick in, get fit and be a cop. In the meantime, she'd be spending a few hours sitting in a car with Michael Turner, who fancied her something rotten. She couldn't muster the same level of enthusiasm for him as he had for her. Nice enough guy but dull, geeky and obsessed with football. Debbie was polite and friendly but struggled to stay awake sometimes.

They were two hours into their vigil. Conversation well and truly dried.

"You want a cup of tea?"

"Aye, go on then."

Michael reached into the back and extracted his flask from a holdall. It had two cups fitted Russian Doll-like to the top. He poured a steaming brew into one and handed it to Debbie. Watching her sip, he fantasised about those lips sipping on his steaming brew. Debbie Does Mickey. The daydreaming caused a stirring in his trousers and enough of a distraction to allow him to overfill his own cup; spilling over the edge, scalding his leg, causing him to yelp in pain and jump out of his seat. This in turn caused Debbie to start in fright and also spill some of her drink down herself.

"Oh, for fuck's sake! Sorry Debbie. Really sorry."

"Jesus, Michael! Pay attention to what you're doing will you!"

They both got out of the car, wiping themselves down and trying to find some kind of material to dry off the seats.

"You got any tissues or a cloth or anything?"

"Em, aye, I think I do."

Michael rummaged about in the holdall. He always carried some tissue with him. You never knew when the urge to knock one out might strike – especially with the delectable Debbie around. Not only that but they could spend long hours sitting about in one place, and that place might not have access to a fully equipped lavatory.

Debbie stopped rummaging through her own pockets and bag and looked toward the house. A figure, dressed in casual sports clothing, with cap pulled down tight and scarf covering their face, was walking away from the garden gate.

"Hi, hello? Excuse me?" shouted Debbie.

The man stopped, looked at her for an instant, then bolted.

Debbie followed suit. "Michael, come on, he's going to get away!"

By the time Michael reacted, Debbie was in hot pursuit. He slammed the car door and set off after her.

"Debbie, wait for me, what the hell's going on?"

The cap and scarf was a whippet, opening up a sizeable gap on Debbie in no time. When he scaled an eight foot high fence like Spiderman on amphetamines, she was beat. Michael made a comical attempt to follow but, after three aborted attempts to make it over himself, followed by a hand up for Debbie, who also failed to cross, they threw in the towel and trudged back to the car.

"Ok, you were having a cup of tea, Turner spilled some, then so did you and, while this fuckin pantomime was going on, you failed to notice somebody approaching the house?"

"Yes, sir." Debbie nodded, struggling to control the liquid emotion straining to be let loose from her tear ducts. This was an unmitigated disaster. Her father would be furious, mainly because he'd become the butt of relentless piss-taking as soon as this became common knowledge.

Stark raised his eyes to the heavens and shook his head.

"So, what did this guy look like then?"

"A typical Ned, sir. Burberry cap and scarf, shell suit, which was mainly black with some red on it."

"Height? Build? Distinguishing features?"

"Not a big guy, under six feet for sure, normal build I would say, definitely not fat. He was really quick sir, he'd have given Usain Bolt a run for his money, eh."

This attempt at levity fell on pissed off ears.

"You didn't get a look at his face then?"

"No sir, his cap was pulled right down and the scarf was pulled up over his mouth and nose."

"And he'd definitely been up at the door?"

"I think so, I can't be sure. When I saw him, he was at the gate, coming out."

"What about you, Turner? Did you see anything?"

"No, sir. Sorry, sir. I didn't."

Michael Turner returned to looking at his feet and shuffling. Cursing his misfortune, acutely aware that whatever slim chance he had of getting into Debbie's pants, was now down the drain, alongside the remnants of his bastard, Judas of a flask.

Stark left the two youngsters standing next to their car. He actually felt a little sorry for them, even if he couldn't show it.

He walked up the path toward the McDuff's front door, nothing obviously amiss on his approach. The neighbour's dog was going mental, barking incessantly. The garden was a bit scruffy, as he would have expected. Fence in need of paint, grass pleading for a once over with a mower, paving slabs edged with moss. He studied the door itself. Again, nothing struck him as unusual.

The lock was a standard Yale and before leaving the station, Stella gave him her key. Putting on his gloves, he inserted the key and carefully turned it, pushing the door open a tiny fraction at first and looking in. Still nothing looked suspicious. He pushed the door wide enough to allow him access. A pile of mail swished as it shifted. Stark stepped inside.

The house smelled musty, dirty. Clothes and other household items were strewn across most of the floors and surfaces he could see. He sifted the mail, dropping obvious bills and circulars into one evidence bag, and everything else into another. Satisfied, Stark went back outside, closing the door behind himself.

"Right, I'm going to leave you pair to watch over the house again. Do you think you can manage not to make a balls-up of it this time?"

"Yes, sir," replied Debbie.

"Turner?"

140

"Yes, sir."

"OK, make sure you call in anything suspicious right away. Understood?"

"Yes, sir," they said in unison.

Stark got into his car and drove off.

Debbie turned to Michael, "Thanks a fuckin million, Michael! Don't talk to me unless it's something to do with work. Got it?"

He nodded and they got back into their car. Both of them sitting in damp patches.

21. TAKING NOTES

As Billy predicted, the mail mostly consisted of a mixture of begging letters and junk but amongst the begging letters was one with a particularly aggressive approach to receiving a hand out from the lucky winners.

> *I know you won the lottery.*
> *I want two million quid or you will never see your son again.*
> *I'll be in touch soon to tell you what to do.*
> *No police or else.*

Stella was sitting in the interview room, sipping tea from a styrofoam cup, the welt on her face bruising up nicely. Her nose stopped leaking blood but replaced it with snot to accompany her tears. The initial hysteria upon reading the ransom note had subsided but she was still shaking from the shock, crying softly.

Stark and McGhee sat opposite her, waiting for the chance to resume questioning. McGhee had briefed his superiors who'd given the go ahead to treat the investigation as a kidnapping, as opposed to a missing persons. The note seemed genuine and was hardly an unexpected turn of events. Most of the cops had been bracing themselves for exactly this scenario.

"I know this is really tough to deal with Stella but we can only help Jack if you talk to us," said McGhee.

"I don't want to talk, I want to give this piece of shit

nutcase the money an' get my boy back."

"I can understand that Stella but we really want to catch this guy, stop him doing anything like this again."

"That's no' my problem, eh. I want to pay up an' be done wi' it. Poor wee Jack must be terrified."

"He'll be ok if we play this the right way. We need to let the kidnapper think we're doing exactly what he wants but we'll be ready to grab him the second he makes a mistake. And he will make a mistake, I'm sure of it."

"Look, I'm no' going to tell you again. I'm paying. It's only money. I don't want you lot playing about wi' my laddie's life. Got it?"

Stella's emotions shifted away from despair, firmly toward indignant anger. This was an affront. People always say money can't buy you happiness. She used to think only folk who had plenty would say something stupid like that, but she was beginning to believe they might be right. The lottery win was a curse. All her hopes of a new life, a new start, being ripped apart.

"Have you any idea who might be behind this? Any enemies or folk holding grudges that you know about?"

"No, I can't think of anyone in particular. Let's be honest, Detective Stark, when it comes to money like I've just won, there's going to be no shortage of greedy bastards hoping to get their hands on a bit of it, eh."

"Aye, I suppose. What about Billy? He must have made a few enemies along the way?"

"What, like you, you mean?" Stella sneered and McGhee gave Stark a puzzled look. "Aye, Billy has put a few noses out of joint – literally in some cases – but folk round our way are shite scared from him an' Malky. Whoever this is can't know who they're dealing wi'."

A fair point thought Stark. He wondered if anyone from the Bottom End would have the bottle to try and extort money from Billy McDuff. Maybe they were looking for an outsider, an opportunist. If it was somebody local, they'd have to be pretty desperate or suicidally avaricious.

"What about the money, Stella? Billy says you stole it. Is that right?"

"Is it fuck! That was my ticket, paid for wi' my money. It's my money an' it's up to me what I do wi' it."

The rights or wrongs of lottery ticket ownership wasn't really any kind of priority for the cops at the moment.

"Ok, there's also the small matter of that assault earlier on. Do you want to press charges?"

"No, it's no' worth the grief. I kind of understand it anyway. If he'd done the same to me, I might have tried to punch his lights out as well, eh."

"Right, well, if you're sure?"

"Aye, positive."

"Well, I think we'll leave it there for now, Stella. Go home, get some rest and we'll be back in touch about how to proceed," said McGhee.

"Home? That will be right. What Billy did today was just for starters. If you lot hadn't been there, I'd be in the hospital, minimum. I need to be somewhere else other than in that house."

"Ok, but we need to know where you are. Give us your mobile number so we can get in touch if anything happens. We'll be keeping Billy in for the night but might have to let him go tomorrow. We'll let you know in advance if he's let out."

"Right, fine. But, just so's we're clear, I'm paying this bastard to get wee Jack back, got it?"

"Aye, we've got it, Stella. Like I say, we'll be in touch."

The briefing room was far livelier than it'd been the first time McGhee addressed the massed ranks.

"Right then, let's get started. I don't think it's a massive turn up for the books that winning a lottery jackpot has attracted the wrong kind of attention. We need to work fast to find out who's behind the abduction of Jack McDuff and stop them doing anything too drastic to the poor wee bugger."

"Are the parents keen on paying up, sir?"

"Aye, DC Barr, they are and I can't blame them. If it was me, I'd be the same. It's only money and they'll still have plenty left if they do pay this ransom demand. However, there's always a chance that paying this kidnapper what he wants the first time won't be enough. He might get greedy, try for more. Whatever way it pans out, our job is to make sure the laddie gets home safe and the bastard who's taken him doesn't get away wi' a load of cash."

DCI McLaren walked into the room with Chief Superintendent Matthews and a hush descended.

"Carry on, Jim, I'll talk to the lads and lasses in a minute," said Matthews.

"Thank you, sir. Given the gravity of the situation, we'll be bringing in some specialist help. A psych profiler from Glasgow is on their way, along with one of their lads with training in hostage negotiation. Other than that, it'll be hard graft. Door to door, checking CCTV, foot patrols and a whole load of interviews. I'll still be heading up on the ground but Chief Matthews will be assuming overall responsibility and working with DCI McLaren to handle the press and so on.

"Does anybody have any questions so far?"

Eyes flicked sideways, lips pursed, arms folded and unfolded, pencils tapped and nobody spoke. Stark looked up to find McLaren giving him a slit-eyed stare. He smiled and the senior man grimaced, looking away. Stark's new best pal handed over to the Chief.

"Thanks, Jim. As you know, a case of this nature will be big news. We're going to have the media all over it like a rash. The important thing is to keep developments and leads in house. We don't need any bloody leaks. I don't want them getting the tiniest scrap that hasn't been vetted first. Am I clear?"

Assent circulated in various forms, including

resentment at the inference.

"Good. I'll leave you in the capable hands of DI McGhee and look forward to getting a result. Let's get this wee boy back to his folks as soon as we can. Thanks."

With that, the two senior officers departed and the tasks and duties got doled out.

McGhee left Stark until last.

"Right, Adam, me and you are going to have a wee word with the laddie's coach."

"What about Billy McDuff?"

"Letting him cool off. The doctor says he'll need a couple of hours to recover his speech and get back on an even keel after the spray. Need to try and keep him away from his wife for now as well. Things are going to be tricky enough without that domestic nonsense getting in the way."

"OK, fair enough. Is the coach here then?"

"No, but a couple of the lassies have gone off to get him. Let's get a cup of tea, spend a few minutes reviewing the stuff we've got so far."

***

Cammy was vaguely aware of the phone ringing but much more aware of the pounding between his temples. He rolled over, his stomach lurched, but he checked the release of its contents. Just.

It was his mother. The recognition swept away the murk in his head.

"Ma?"

"Aye, Cammy, it's me. Where are you?"

"In my bed, where are you?"

"I can't tell you the now, son."

"What do you mean you can't tell me?"

"Never mind that, have you heard from your brother or your Da today?"

"Naw, how?"

"Look, there's no easy way of saying this, eh. Jack's been kidnapped. Held to ransom for some of the money I won on the lottery."

"Jesus, fuckin, Christ! What the fuck's going on, Ma? You have won the lottery then?"

"Aye."

"How come you've buggered off then?"

"It's complicated."

"Who the fuck's got Jack?"

"We don't know yet, son. The polis are looking for the guy. He sent a note demanding a load of money."

Cammy's addled mind struggled to keep up with the flow of conversation.

"Don't worry though, I'm going to pay up, get wee Jack back as soon as we can, eh."

"Ma, this is fucked up. Where's Da?"

"He's in the cells. Gave me a hiding an' the polis pepper sprayed him."

Cammy got out of bed, started pacing the floor of his bedroom.

"Holy shit, that's no' good."

"No, son, it isn't. Look, I'm with your Auntie Maureen. I can't tell you where we are until your Da's calmed down a bit."

"Fuck's sake Ma, what am I supposed to do? I've no money, Da's in the nick, an' you're off fuck knows where. There's no' a scrap of food in the house, an' I've no' got any clean clothes. Jesus, fuckin, wept. This isn't right."

Stella's scalp prickled; the itch of her guilt.

"Alright, son. I'm sorry. I gave your Da a pile of cash to look after you with. The useless bastard hasn't even been to the shops then?"

"Naw, he's been to the fuckin pub though, eh."

"The selfish prick!"

"That's good coming from you. Win the lottery an' instantly fuck off wi' the money, leaving me an' Jack to it. Selfish doesn't even come close."

148

Stella swallowed hard as tears threatened to flow.

"Ok, I'm sorry, let's meet up, son. I'll get you some money an' you can buy food an' some new clothes. Bring your washing wi' you, an' me an' your Auntie Maureen will sort it out."

"Right. I'm going to get a shower. Phone me back in about fifteen minutes."

"Alright son, cheerio the now."

The line went dead. Stella sat down heavily on the hotel bed, dropping the phone to her side. Crushing exhaustion squeezed the breath from her lungs in gasps. Her muscles felt tied down, attached to a pulley system, inexorably dragging her to the floor.

William stood up from his chair in the corner of the suite. "I'll go and see Cammy for you, Mum. You're done in. The last thing you need the now is more grief from that ungrateful wee bastard."

Stella looked up, baleful, wet eyes taking William's gaze.

"Ok son, thanks. You're right, I'm absolutely shattered."

She reached into her handbag and withdrew a large roll of banknotes. Without counting, why bother, she peeled off a portion and handed it to William.

"Now, please, William, don't be getting into any fights wi' Cammy. Just give him the cash an' get back here as soon as you can. Your wee brother has some pretty dodgy mates these days, an' I don't want you ending up in the hospital. D'you hear me, son?"

"Aye Mum, don't worry. I'm a lover no' a fighter!"

They both laughed as William closed the door behind him.

William and Cammy arranged to meet in the Cross Words car park. Public but private at the same time. William arrived early, Cammy arrived late.

"Where the fuck have you been?"

Cammy scowled at his older brother. "Fuck off, you

said ten to, it's only five past you prick."

"Look you wee wank, I'm doing you a favour, no' the other way about. Here!"

William shoved the money into Cammy's chest. His younger brother instinctively grabbed it, dropping the holdall containing his dirty clothes to the ground in the process.

"If it was up to me, you'd be getting fuck all. What did you ever do for Ma except give her grief?"

"Ach, fuckin rap it, William. This has got fuck all to do wi' you, eh."

"Oh, an' if you think I'm taking that back to Ma for her to do," said William, pointing at the bag, "you're sadly mistaken."

"What? Ma said she'd do it for me. I don't have a clue how to use the washing machine. Just take it you fuckin bentshot!"

William grabbed Cammy by the scruff, taking him by surprise with the strength of his grip.

"I might well be a fuckin bentshot, Cammy, but I don't take shit about it from the likes of you any more. You can take your washing to the laundrette, or you can chuck it in the bin for all I care; just take the money, and that bag, an' fuck off out of my sight."

He pushed his brother forcefully away causing him to stumble and fall on his backside, scattering money in the process. Cammy scrambled about trying to prevent any of the precious notes from being blown off down the high street.

"Bastard! Fuck you, gayboy! This isn't finished. I'll see you around!" roared Cammy in frustration.

William got into his car, opened the window, and blew Cammy a kiss before driving off.

22. PAYBACK

"Aye, I'm sorry, sir, no' really sure how it got missed on that first look through the letters, eh." said Barr quietly.

McGhee and Stark, just back from a fruitless half hour interviewing Edgars Balodis, looked at the plastic bag, reading and re-reading the short, angry note it contained.

McDuff,

You are scum! How dare you talk about my son like that. He's a real person, with a real disease and you ignorant low-lives have no right keeping all that money to spend on drugs and flash cars and all that other superficial shit you're bound to blow it on. How would you feel if someone did something horrible to your son? If my son dies because you wouldn't lend me that money in time, maybe you'll find out?

I'm not scared of you. I've faced the worst that life could ever throw at me.

Your neighbour

"Right, well, at least we've got it now. Have the lab boys had a look?" asked McGhee.

Barr shuffled his feet, looked at the floor before looking straight at Stark.

"Just about to take it down there now, but thought

151

you'd want a look first, sir."

Again the shuffle followed by the re-focus.

"Thing is, sir, I think I know who wrote this."

"What?"

"You know how I told you my wife Kirsty's a social worker?"

"Aye."

"Well, she helps look after a guy down in the scheme who has a terminally ill son. A wee bairn about a year old I think. Some kind of genetic disorder. The guy's been fundraising to try and take him to America for this special treatment they've got over there. His name's Greg Marshall."

The two senior officers looked at each other.

"Ok, Barr, take a PC with you, get down there and bring this guy in. It looks like we might just have found our kidnapper," said McGhee.

Greg Marshall looked bewildered, obviously experiencing arrest and interview for the first time. Stark and McGhee sat opposite him. With formalities regarding rights and recordings completed, McGhee took the lead.

"Mr Marshall, you understand why we've brought you in don't you?"

"No, not really, the cop who arrested me said something about kidnap and extortion. I mean, I couldn't take it in. I just thought it was a mistake an' it would all be sorted out once I got here, eh."

"Really? That's the best you can come up with? That you know nothing about the abduction of Jack McDuff and subsequent demand for money with menaces?"

The colour drained from Greg's face at the mention of the name McDuff. "I, I, oh god! It's that note isn't it, the one I sent them after they abused wee Brandon. Is that what this is about? Coz I never meant it, I was just boiling angry after they called me an' Brandon all sorts of horrible names when I asked for some money to get him to

152

America."

"So, you admit to writing this note then?" said McGhee, pushing it across the table.

"Oh shit, oh fuck, yes, yes, I did write that note but I swear it was just the drink talking. I got pissed, I was furious an' I just vented. I didn't mean I was really going to hurt their laddie. I know it looks bad, especially if you're saying somebody has actually kidnapped him, but I would never hurt a child, never!

"Oh, god, Brandon, he's got nobody else, what will happen if I go to jail? Can I go to jail for writing this? Can I? Oh, Brandon, I'm so sorry!" Greg's emotions burst like a breached dam.

"Mr Marshall, please, try to remain calm. We're following a few lines of enquiry at the moment," said McGhee. "Clearly, writing this letter was not the smartest thing you could have done, regardless of whether you kidnapped Jack McDuff or not, and technically, yes, it may constitute a crime in its own right. But, let's leave that to one side for now. Where were you on Wednesday evening between seven and nine pm?"

Greg wiped his face with his sleeve, tried to compose himself.

"I was...I think I was...no I was definitely in the house. I'm nearly always in the house during the evening. Looking after Brandon is a full-time job. I don't have a social life, I don't get time off from him."

"So, what about just now? Who's looking after him for you while you're in here with us?" asked Stark.

"My sister, Jackie. She lives in Alva. I called her an' told her it was an emergency. She came over to watch him, eh."

"And does she watch him for you often?"

"No, hardly ever. Jackie's got her own life, her own kids. It's hard, she's a good person but she struggles to cope with Brandon, avoids babysitting him unless I'm totally desperate. I understand, it's a terrible thing. I don't judge her for it."

"I assume she'll confirm that you never asked her to babysit on Wednesday?"

"Yes."

"And, is there anyone else who helps out?"

"No, my folks are both dead, my wife died in labour and her folks are down in Devon. I saw them at Christmas for a couple of days, but that's all. There's just my sister left."

Once again, emotion threatened to overcome Greg.

"Oh, and can I assume that was you running away from the Community Wardens after posting this note?"

"Aye, sorry, that was me. I just panicked. I knew it was wrong but I couldn't help myself."

"So, where was Brandon, while you were playing postie?" asked McGhee.

"In my car a street away. After I gave those two wardens the slip, I ditched my hat and scarf and doubled back. He wasn't alone for more than about ten minutes."

The two cops looked at each other and nodded.

"Ok, let's stop there for now. We'll reconvene in a while, Mr Marshall."

Outside the interview room Stark and McGhee stopped at the coffee machine for McGhee to partake of the decidedly average fare it dispensed.

"What do you think then, Adam?"

"I'm inclined to believe him. He's no' got the time or the bottle to go after Billy McDuff, or his laddie. I think he did get some Dutch courage, wrote that note an' then hoped to fuck McDuff never found out it was him."

"Aye, I'm inclined to agree but I'm no' ruling him out just yet. I've seen folks like him before. Crocodile tears, turn on the waterworks, reel off sob stories, try to look sorry, devastated or pathetic but all the time, they're at it. Let's leave him to stew for a bit, then let him go, under caution. I'll get DC Barr to do the honours in about an hour."

"Sounds good."

"Meanwhile, we can finish off interviewing Billy, now he's recovered from his hot shower."

"Right you are, lead on McDuff!"

McGhee looked at him with an arched eyebrow and shook his head.

"Aye, alright, but I've been waiting to use that for days now!" protested Stark.

They both laughed.

"Jeezo, Adam, you're patter's fuckin chronic. Maybe I should send you back out on the door to door like McLaren wanted?"

***

Billy was incandescent. Bloody Adam Stark. Getting pepper-sprayed by any cop would have been infuriating, but to have that dick administer the punishment...

Stark would get his, Billy would make sure of it. As for the bitch that was his wife, she'd be well advised to stay away from him for quite some time – after she'd handed over a huge wad of cash first. Walking away from the police station, he dialled Malky's number; still through to voicemail.

"Malky, for fuck's sake, get back to me. I need to know what the fuck's going on."

Billy headed for the supermarket, cigarettes and booze calling his name. Suitably stocked up and ignoring the funny looks a few folk gave him, he headed for the taxi rank.

"Billy!"

He looked behind him. Davey McLatchey waving, picking up pace, trying to catch up.

"Billy, wait the now."

He stopped, let Davey close the gap between them. It transpired Davey was a bit worse for drink and not in the best physical condition either. Air creaked and rattled out of his lungs like a badly oiled hinge on a storm shutter. Sweat glistened on his skin, a couple of wayward strands of hair glued across his brow.

"Aye, what is it, Davey? I'm in a bit of a hurry," Billy lied.

"Just wanted to say, I heard wee Jack's gone missing. I'm just wanting to offer youse my services if youse need somebody to help look for him, eh."

Billy looked Davey up and down. A harmless wee guy really, ravaged by years of neglect and alcohol. When they lost their jobs at the Brewery, Billy coped a lot better than Davey did. No family, no steadying influence, abandoned by the rest of society and lost in the system, he slowly fell apart. His heart was in the right place but it was marooned in the wrong body.

"Aye, that's good of you to offer Davey but we'll manage, thanks. How are you doing these days anyway. You're looking well."

Davey grinned.

"Cheers, Bill. Aye, I'm doing ok my man, doing ok. Gagging for a wee drink mind you, but nothing new there, eh?"

They both laughed.

"Ah, Davey, man, you're a funny wee cunt, so you are. Here, get yourself a drink on me, mate."

Billy pushed a twenty pound note into Davey's top pocket.

"You're a fuckin gent, Billy McDuff. A fuckin gen-tel-man! I hope you find the wee fellah soon an' I meant what I said. Anything you need, you just ask me, eh."

"No bother, Davey. Got to go mate, I'll see you around. Cheers."

The taxi pulled up behind a marked car. Billy paid the driver, marched straight up to the soporific community wardens and banged on the window. Michael Turner almost soiled himself before getting out to confront Billy.

Debbie Lynch quickly followed suit.

"What do you think you're doing, sir?"

"Never mind that son, what are you pair doing sitting outside my fuckin house?" said Billy, getting right in Turner's face.

"Please watch your language, sir. And please step back from me. I take it you're Mr McDuff?"

"Aye, an' who the fuck are you two, an' why are you watching my house?"

"Sir, please don't swear at me again or I'll be forced to call for assistance. We're community wardens and we've been asked to watch the house in case your son came back of his own accord, and also watch for anyone suspicious approaching your property."

Turner felt himself shaking. McDuff was an intimidating character so close up, Turner well aware of his reputation locally. Debbie kept the width of the vehicle bonnet between her and Billy. She too knew who he was, what he might be capable of.

"Right, well, I'm home now, so you can piss off. I don't need babysitting an' if Jack does come back, I'll be here."

"I'll need to check this out, sir. They may ask us to stay."

Billy growled in disapproval, before walking off up the path and into his house.

"Fuck's sake Debbie, thanks for your back up!"

"Aye right, Michael, piss off. Give the boss a bell an' see if we can get out of here. I'm bored shitless an' the thought of having to deal wi' that psycho again isn't exactly appealing."

Turner made the call. Confirmation came through that they could stand down for now, so they drove back to the station for re-assignment, in silence.

***

Cammy stood in the doorway waiting; fear and excitement

whirling through his senses in a way he'd only previously experienced riding the biggest of fairground roller-coasters. Looking at his phone for the umpteenth time, seconds began passing between glances instead of minutes. Finally, just when he was about to lose hope that Badger's contact would show, a car drew up.

The blacked out passenger window of the Subaru Imprezza slid down, the guy seated behind it nodded.

"You Cammy then?"

"Aye."

"Got the money?"

"Aye, you got the merchandise?"

The shaven-headed man nodded again. "Get in the back."

Cammy looked left and right, then did as he was told. As soon as the door clunked shut, the car roared off, tyres squealing, pinning Cammy to the seat. Back on the rollercoaster.

Twenty minutes later they came to a screeching halt and the guy in the front seat turned round. He pulled back the corner of the cloth package in his hands, revealing a gun.

"9mm Glock, full clip, untraceable. A quality bit of kit, my man."

Cammy was uninitiated in the ways of guns, his only knowledge gleaned from computer games and movies. He'd heard of a Glock though, it sounded just the ticket.

"Aye, spot on mate. How much?"

"Four hundred."

"What? Badger told me it would be nearer two."

"Aye, well, Badger's a clueless wee knob. And so are you, if you think you're getting a fully loaded, untraceable Glock for two hundred quid."

"Alright, I'll take it."

Cammy had the money ready. He knew they'd want four hundred but thought he'd play dumb, chance his arm. No point pushing it though. These two were serious guys who wouldn't take kindly to piss-ripping and he had plenty of money, with plenty more on its way. Cammy handed over the cash and took the cloth-wrapped gun, shoving it under his tracksuit jacket.

"Is it all there?" asked the driver; another shaven-headed hard man.

"Aye."

"Right, wee man, out you get."

"What? You no' giving me a run back? Where are we?"

"Never mind that, just get the fuck out the motor. How you get home is your business. I couldn't give a fuck. Cheers."

Stepping out of the car, he barely closed the door before it roared off. Cammy looked around. Great, middle of bloody nowhere. He called a taxi and made the call to Badger to set things up at the park. Today was going to be a big day.

The taxi dropped Cammy at the park entrance. Strolling through to the play area, confidence and bravado oozed from him.

Cammy removed the gun from the cloth, tucking it into the waistband of his trousers. Now he knew why guys got respect for carrying a gun. The shell-suited avenger - all-powerful, untouchable, brimming over with dark, vengeful thoughts.

"Oh aye, look who it isn't - Richard Branson. Or should I just call you Virgin Dick?"

Bart collapsed in self-congratulatory laughter. As Cammy approached he stood up, cracking his knuckles threateningly. Cammy didn't feel threatened, he felt ready.

"Fuck you, Bart. You're the one named after an annoying, wee, yellow prick, eh."

"What did you just say? You think you're a funny cunt do you, McDuff? I thought you'd learned the hard way no' to mess wi' me, but maybe I'll just need to remind you, eh? And what the fuck are you laughing at Badger, you useless fat bastard?"

Simpson punched Badger in the chest, knocking the wind from him, before advancing on Cammy. When he got within six feet, Cammy produced the gun.

"What the fuck?"

"On your fuckin knees, Simpson, now!"

Bart stopped, hands on hips, shaking his head.

"What's that, McDuff? A fuckin spud gun?"

Cammy let off a round which thudded into the ground beside Bart's feet, the power of the kick taking him by surprise, the effect on Simpson dramatic. Bart obeyed the order to kneel, cowering and whimpering as he did so.

"Cammy, please, I was only kidding, don't shoot me for fuck's sake."

Cammy brought the gun round, smashing it into the side of Bart's face, sending him to the ground in a heap. He climbed on top of the prone Simpson and moved in very close to his ear, aping his erstwhile tormentor's attack on him.

"How does it feel, Bart? You reckoned you could push me about, make threats, get my lottery money off me. Well, I've got news for you cunto, the only thing you're getting from me is a bullet in the head."

"Cammy, please, stop, I'm sorry, I don't want your money. Please. I'm sorry, I'm sorry, I'm sorry!"

"Too late for that, prickface. Say goodbye!"

Cammy pushed the gun against Simpson's temple who screamed like a little girl. Cammy glanced up at Badger and winked. Then, leaning in close, he shouted.

"BANG!"

Simpson recoiled from the noise, pissing his trousers in the process. As Cammy stood back, Simpson scrambled to his feet and ran.

"Aye, run home to your Mammy and ask her to change your nappy you fuckin wanker!"

Cammy and Badger also pissed themselves, but only in the laughing-like-fuck sense of the phrase.

***

Billy snapped awake. He'd nodded off during the fourth beer, the film he'd chosen proving inadequately violent or entertaining enough to maintain consciousness.

"Billy."

He shot bolt upright out of his chair, spilling the remainder of the can down his front and onto the carpet. Wrestling the figure in front of him to the ground, he started pummelling. Questions could come later.

"Billy, Billy, for fuck's sake bro, pack it in, it's me, Malky!"

Billy stopped and got up, his vision and thoughts clearing.

"Malky, what the fuck are you playing at? Where've you been an' what the fuck are you doing sneaking up on me while I'm sleeping, eh?"

Malky pushed himself backwards, up onto the settee, rubbing his jaw and arms, which took the brunt of Billy's blows.

"I've been out an' about, ken. But I've hit a bit of a snag, bro."

"A snag? What does that mean?"

"You mind when we split up last week after the pub? You should do, you gave me a fuckin doing then an' all."

"Aye, I mind. How, what about it?"

"Well, I was just about to go into my flat when this fuckin nutter attacked me. No' got a clue where he came from. Just as well I've got the reflexes of a fuckin cat. Cunt slipped at the vital moment, I connected, he went down like a sack of spuds an' fuckin died, eh."

"What? Did you just say he fuckin died?"

"Aye, it wasn't my fault Billy, I hardly touched the fucker. He fell an' banged his head on the steps."

"Oh, that's just fuckin brilliant, Malky. Wait a minute, that was last week. What the fuck? How did you no' tell me about this before now?"

"I was trying to deal wi' it, sort it without involving you."

"I can't believe this, Malky. Only you could manage to fuck things up so badly. What have I told you about that temper!"

"I told you, it wasn't me started it. He tried to jump me. It was an accident. You saw the state of me that night, I could hardly bite my own lip, eh."

Billy cracked open a new can and swigged deeply from it.

"Can I get one of them?"

"In the fridge. Help yourself, it's what you normally do."

Malky ignored the barb, returned with his refreshment and sat back down.

"Look, Billy, it's ok. I've buried him. Nobody will find the body, I've made sure of that."

"Who was he? Did you know him?"

"Naw, young guy, late teens, early twenties maybe. No id on him. All ninja'd up in black. I didn't recognise him from anywhere either."

"That's just fuckin weird. Where did you bury him?"

"I'm no' telling you, Billy. The less you know, the less you can get into bother for. *It's* sorted, but I'm no'."

Billy shook his head and got himself another beer, the first having gone by the wayside in a matter of four or five gulps.

"I'm going to need more money, Billy. Enough to get away abroad. Spain, the Bahamas, somewhere well away from here, eh."

"You're a greedy wee cunt, Malky. I knew this would happen. Soon as there's a sniff of big money, you want more. I bet there was no fuckin young guy attacked you, you've made this up to get a bigger share. You must think I'm some fuckin soft touch, eh."

Malky leapt out of his chair, started stomping around the room.

"Fuck you, Billy! You're the greedy cunt! An ungrateful, greedy cunt at that. I saved you jail time back in '98, took the rap for you. Now, some guy attacks me, an' instead of backing me up, you're calling me all sorts an' getting all shitty about it. Fuck you!"

"There we go! I wondered how long it would be before you cast that up again. I've paid you back many times over for that Malky, an' no' just wi' cash. Stop shouting the odds or somebody's going to hear you."

They stopped shouting but tension took its place, humming like an exposed power cable. After a couple of minutes, Billy spoke again.

"You need to take me to the body. I don't give a fuck about being involved, it needs sorted; but I need proof."

"Fine, whatever, get a coat. Oh, an' you'll need boots, it's pretty muddy."

23. BAD LUCK AND TROUBLE

"Listen, son, there's something I've been meaning to tell you for a wee while now."

Stark put down his mug of tea and looked at his mother; a butterfly flutter of unease.

"For about the last six months I've no' been keeping very well. The doctors did a load of tests but couldn't seem to find out what was up. Then, about a month ago, one of the tests showed..." Mary caught her breath and her eyes filled, "...cancer."

"Oh Jesus, Ma, is that why you were being sick the other night?"

Stark got up and embraced his mother, feeling the bag of bones she'd become, panic coursing through him. All those dark thoughts confirmed but he needed to hold it together. It wouldn't do his mother any good to see his pain; she had enough of her own to cope with.

"Aye, that's right, but please, Adam, no' so tight son, eh."

"Christ, sorry, Ma." He let her go.

Stark didn't want to ask the next question but he needed to, had to know.

"What's the prognosis?"

Mary shook her head a tear spilling from her left eye, bottom lip wobbling. "It's terminal son, six months maybe, they're no' totally sure."

"No, that can't be right. Have you had a second

opinion?"

"I don't need one, Adam. It is what it is. It's my time."

"No, I can pay for a private doctor, we'll get you whatever treatment you need."

Mary took his hands in hers and looked at him, starting to regain her strength, her usual resolve. That was the hardest part over with and he'd taken it pretty well considering. "Adam, it's all through me and it's malignant. They offered me a load of drastic treatments but I've turned them down."

"What?"

"Look, son, I don't want to spend what time I've got left attached to machines, having needles shoved into me over and over and suffering all those horrible side-effects. It's no use, it's too late. I've accepted it, I'm at peace with it. I'll take the pain killers but that's it."

Stark wanted to shout at her, convince her to change her mind but he knew she was right. He would just have to help her the best he could. He hugged her again, this time being more gentle.

After a few moments, Mary broke free of his grasp.

"Adam, we need to do the best we can wi' this situation. We can't spend the next few months being sad, greetin' our eyes out every ten minutes. I have a short time left. There's a few things I'd like to do. Most of all I want to enjoy myself, pretend everything's fine, carry on as normal until I can't manage that any more, ok?"

Stark nodded and smiled. It made perfect sense to his head and his heart but, in truth, his heart wasn't really convinced.

The pager went off in his pocket. "Oh for fuck's sake!"

"Adam, language, you're no' wi' your pals the now, son!"

"Sorry Ma, I need to go and check this out. Even the polis can't escape the long arm."

He walked out into the back garden and phoned McGhee.

"McGhee?"

"Aye."

"Did you page me?"

"I did indeed. You'll need to come in right away, Adam. There's been a bit of a development."

"What's up, you found the McDuff laddie?"

"Well, not quite. We've got a body, but it's no' Jack."

"Shit! I'll be right there."

Stark met McGhee in the station car park and transferred to a pool car. Rain bounced off the tarmac so hard that the phrase pool car seemed rather aptly ambiguous.

"Fuck me, now that's what I call rain! So, what's the script, Jim?"

"Well, we got a call this morning from a member of the public saying their dog had dug up a body while they were out walking it this morning."

"Where about?"

McGhee fired up the engine and pulled out of the car park.

"Up in the Ochils, near Glen Quay Reservoir, do you know it?"

"No' really, no."

"Anyway, they were pretty distressed, said the body's in a right state. As it happens, we also got a call from that fitba coach Edgars Balodis, the one we talked to about Jack McDuff, mind?"

"Aye, nice guy, didn't add much to what we knew."

"Aye, well, he phoned last night to report his son, Andris, was missing."

"Fuck's sake, what is it wi' folks round here and missing children?"

"Indeed, but of course, it set my alarm bells ringing about this body."

"How long has the Balodis laddie been missing?"asked Stark.

"About two days, but his Dad wasn't too sure. His other son was attacked last week and he's been spending a lot of time at the hospital."

"Attacked and hospitalised? We never got wind of that did we?"

"Naw, they decided no' to pursue it. I'm no' sure the father has much idea what happened. We can follow that up in due course but first things first. We need to get up to this reservoir and have a look at the body."

***

"William, please, just leave it, eh. I hate it when you and your brothers fight."

"But Mum, he's an ungrateful wee shit, an' he gets right on my bloody nerves. You shouldn't give him anything."

Stella sighed and took back her card and then the money from the cash machine.

"It's just money, William. Have you any idea how much stuff six million quid will buy you? More than I could ever need. I don't want loads of stuff, I don't need tons of cash. I just want to get wee Jack out of trouble an' then to get shot of your useless Da. Now, here, go an' give that to Cammy for me. Please."

"Ok, but I think you're mad. He'll never be satisfied, eh. The more you give him, the more he'll spend."

Stella's phone rattled in her bag, vibrating rather than ringing. She took it out and cancelled Billy's call.

"I'm meeting your Auntie Maureen in Stirling for lunch. Once you've sorted Cammy out, we'll meet you outside the Thistle Centre. Just text me to let me know when you're on your way. If something happens with the polis or Jack, I'll let you know, eh."

Arranging to meet in the car park at the Cross Swords again, this time William was late. Cammy, sopping wet, stood under an overhang proving inadequate as a rain shelter. William chuckled to himself. That would teach the wee bastard.

Pulling up alongside his scowling brother, William gestured for him to get into the passenger seat.

"Haha! A bit wet is it, Cammy?"

Enough water dripped off Cammy to give the impression he'd brought the rain inside with him.

"Aye, very funny, gaylord. Where's my money?"

William grabbed at him again. "I fuckin warned you, you little prick. Don't talk to me like that."

Cammy squirmed free in a shower of droplets, producing the gun, aiming it directly in William's face, who pressed back against his door in surprise.

"What the actual fuck, Cammy? Is that thing fuckin loaded? Put it down!"

"Don't tell me what to do you fuckin faggot. Give me the money, an' then get out. I'm borrowing the motor. I've got a wee errand to run."

"What? You can't even drive, you're too young."

"I can drive fine, now give me the money and get out the car. Now!"

William handed over the money, and then stepped out into the downpour. Cammy shuffled across into the driver's seat. After a quick adjustment to the driving position, he careened into the centre of the car park, pulled a handbrake turn, and accelerated; deliberately driving through a huge puddle. The mini tsunami the car tyres created, drenched William.

Cammy stopped, opened the window and blew William a kiss, before driving off.

William fished his phone from his pocket, relieved to find it damp but not ruined.

"Mum?"

"Aye, is that you on your way, son?"

"No it fuckin isn't! You're never going to believe what just happened!"

169

***

The rain was battering down by the time Stark and McGhee turned up the access track to Glen Quay Reservoir. The verdant vegetation a testament to just how often the sky provided liquid refreshment.

The track was a bit rough but McGhee took it slow. Ahead they could see the vehicles of those who'd already arrived, parked on the track verges. They took their place at the back of the queue.

"You got a brolly, Jim?"

"Aye, made sure I put a couple in this morning."

"Thank fuck for that. I thought we were going to get bloody soaked."

They got out and, with umbrellas deployed, walked over to the edge of the track where Ian Barr and a couple of uniforms huddled under their own umbrella.

"What's happening, Barr?" asked McGhee.

"Hi, sir, sir." Barr nodded in recognition of both senior officers. "SOCO are up there just now doing their thing. Looks like one body – young, Caucasian, male. Probably been dead a couple of days."

"Too early for cause I suppose?" asked Stark.

"I think so sir, not had any confirmation from the SOCO guys on that as yet, eh."

"What about the finder?"

"Been taken home, sir. Suffering from shock. A female PC is sitting with her and taking the official statement once she feels up to it."

"How likely she's involved?" asked McGhee.

"Wouldn't think it's likely at all, sir. She's eighty-seven and no' in the best of health. She drives up here an' let's the dog off the lead, let's it run about to get exercise. It wasn't coming back, so she went looking for it in the woods here an' found it chewing on the boy's bones."

"Oof, no wonder she's in shock. She doesn't sound much like a prime suspect though, I'll give you that."

McGhee took Stark over to one side.

"I've been told by McLaren that we've to split up. You're taking this, and I'm sticking with the McDuff laddie's abduction."

"Aye, fair enough, Jim. That makes sense. I tell you what, when I moved up here from the big smoke I thought I'd be in for an easy ride. How wrong was I?"

McGhee laughed. "Aye, it's been a bit full-on right enough."

"Anyway, now that we're clear about who's doing what, I'm going to leave you to come back with DC Barr. I'm heading back to Alloa. I'm a bit surprised there's no' been any more contact from the kidnapper. I thought he'd have been onto the family, looking for a way to get a hold of his dosh."

"Righto, I'll see you back at the nick in due course. Cheers, Jim."

"Aye, cheers."

The SOCO guys were carrying the body out of the woods on a stretcher. Stark approached the senior investigator.

"DI Adam Stark. How's it going?"

"Archie Brown." They shook hands. "It's going ok, considering, thanks. Looks like whoever did this, did it in stages. Victim's a young male, Caucasian, between eighteen and twenty-five years old. Head trauma was probable cause of death. Blow to the back of the head but it's too early to tell what with. It looks to me like he was buried once, then dug up again and reburied."

"Really? That's a bit strange is it no'?"

"It is, yes, but I think the clowns responsible have been watching too much TV."

"What do you mean?"

"Well, they seem to have come back to remove his teeth and fingers in some stupid attempt to prevent us identifying him."

"Hang on, you said they, how do you know there was

171

more than one person involved?"

"Oh, when I said they were clowns, I wasn't kidding. They left two distinct sets of footprints in the mud around the grave."

Stark shook his head. "Oh dear, that wasn't too bright now was it?"

"No DI Stark, it certainly wasn't. I don't think you're dealing with criminal masterminds here. I'll be in touch once we've done the autopsy."

"Aye, ok, thanks. Just one thing to let you know. We might have a lead on the victim already. Young Latvian guy has been posted missing by his Dad and this body might fit the bill."

"Ok, I'll be sure to make the boy presentable after the autopsy for any formal id you need to do."

"Cheers, Archie. Appreciate that. Here's my card."

The SOCO team finished loading the body into the ambulance and the cavalcade departed, leaving the woods to the birds and the rain. Stark retreated to his own thoughts as Barr drove them back to Alloa.

**

Malky switched on the telly in Billy's front room. The local news was on.

"Police in Alloa have confirmed that the body of a young man was discovered early this morning in the Ochil Hills near Glendevon. According to a statement, a local woman, out walking her dog, discovered the remains at about seven o'clock. There are no further details at the moment but police say they are treating the death as suspicious.

"Let's go over to our correspondent, Pardeep Anwar, who's live at the scene. Pardeep, what more can you tell us?"

Of course, the answer to that was fuck all, other than it was still raining and he was getting wet. Modern news reporting really was riddled with time-slot-filling, pointless, repetitious shite. Malky switched the TV off, sat back in his chair heavily.

A dog walker. A fucking, interfering, nosey bastard, dog walker. Who else would it be?

"FUCK!"

Billy walked in from the kitchen, clutching a freshly made sausage sandwich.

"What's up wi' you?"

"Aw, man, I can't fuckin believe this!"

"What, for fuck's sake, what?"

"We've got a pretty big problem, Billy. It's just come on the news; some fucker an' their dog have found the body."

Billy stopped mid-chew, his jaw dropping open to reveal the delightfully compressed mash of bread and meat in his mouth. The string of expletives that followed was potentially worth contacting the people at Guinness World Records about.

"This changes everything, Malky. We need to get the money an' get the fuck out of Dodge as soon as. Taking the dead guy's teeth an' fingers might slow the polis down a bit but they'll work it out eventually. We've no' exactly been careful about the evidence an' the forensics. You managed to convince me nobody would look up there, what a fuckin mistake that was."

"Look Billy, I know that. I'm no' a fuckin moron, eh."

"Really? I'm no' so fuckin sure, eh."

"Aw, fuck off Billy, you thought it was alright an' all, so don't fuckin start on wi' that pish."

"I already decided we needed a new plan. I got Cammy to go an' get us a motor. He should be here soon. We're going to cut out the middle men an' go straight to the source of the cash. We're going to find Stella an' get her to cough up."

"Right you are bro, now that sounds like a proper fuckin plan!"

24. IT'S ALL RELATIVE

"Nice motor, Cammy. Where did you get it?"

"You'll love this Da, I took it from that shirtlifting bastard, William!"

Cammy never saw the punch but he felt it well enough.

"You stupid little fuck! What the fuckin hell were you thinking about, eh? We can expect plod to be round here any minute."

Cammy got up from the floor, rubbing his jaw, feeling sorry for himself.

"But, Da, the bastard was taunting me, I just snapped. He's a dick but he won't go to the polis."

"How do you know that? Jesus Christ, Cammy. Right, well, we're stuck wi' it now, so let's get on wi' this. Give Malky the keys an' let's get on our way. We've got some searching to do."

Cammy's phone started ringing.

"Alright, Ma?"

"Alright? No, I'm no' alright, son. I've just spoken to William, an' he's told me what you did."

"Look, Ma, he asked for it. He was laughing about me getting soaked an' got all arsey about giving me that money. That was after he wouldn't take my washing to you before as well. He's a dickhead."

"You listen to me Cammy, get that car back to William, pronto, or that'll be the last money you'll see from me. Do you hear me? What have I told you about that joy-riding.

175

And a gun? A gun for fuck's sake! You'll get the bloody jail, son."

"Aye, alright, I hear you. It was just a joke, eh. The gun's no' real, it's a fake," he lied.

"Well, it wasn't a very funny joke. William said it looked real to him."

"What the fuck would he know about guns? Anyway, where is he?"

"He's here wi' me in Stirling. We're having lunch wi' your Auntie Maureen in the Thistle Centre, eh. Bring the car to the multi-storey car park an' when you get there, text me, an' we'll come an' meet you to get the keys. Right?"

Stella should have been more careful, guarded. The relaxed nature of her day brought her defences down, causing her to overlook the possibility Cammy might provide a route to Billy.

"Aye, ok. I take it William hasn't called the cops then?"

"No, think yourself lucky. I managed to persuade him to give you a chance to bring it back."

"Ok. He's still a dickhead, but."

"That's enough, son. I'll see you in a wee while an' make sure the polis don't notice you. Cheerio the now."

Cammy put his phone back in his pocket and smiled.

"The search is over Da, I know exactly where Ma is."

"Was that her?"

"Aye. She's in Stirling, wi' Auntie Mo, an' William."

"Is she indeed. Well, let's go pay the three of them a wee visit shall we?"

"Fuckin right bro, time to get our fuckin money!" roared Malky.

"Our fuckin money?" said Billy, frowning.

Malky hesitated just long enough for Billy to snort with laughter.

"Aye, alright, very fuckin good, Billy. Let's go, eh."

***

Edgars Balodis looked like a man whose acquaintance with sleep had become tenuous.

"Thanks for coming in, Mr Balodis," said Stark.

"That is ok. Do you have any news for me detective?"

"Mr Balodis, I'm afraid I need you to prepare yourself for some potentially bad news."

"What does this mean, potentially?"

"Well, you may have heard on the news that a body was discovered this morning in the Ochil Hills. I have to warn you that we think there's a strong possibility that it's your son, Andris."

"Oh dear God," said Edgars quietly, crossing himself as he did so.

"At this stage, we're waiting for the autopsy to be completed, but once it has been, I will contact you to come in and make a formal identification of the body."

"And what if it is not being my son?"

"Well, you'll be very relieved and we'll need to keep trying to find out whose body it is."

"Ok."

"In the meantime, I'd like to ask you some questions."

"Yes, that will be fine."

"Thank you. I know this must be a very hard time for you and your wife. I understand your other son was attacked last week and ended up in hospital."

"Yes."

"Why didn't you or your son report this incident, Mr Balodis? It sounded like a very serious assault."

"Yes, it was serious. He was animal who did this. My son don't see him, so he don't want to say anything to police."

"Where did this assault take place?"

"In Cross Swords pub car park."

Stark admired the man's quiet, stoic manner. No fuss, no drama, just answers.

"Was anyone else involved?"

"My son Juris, he was with friend, Pete. He was hurt

also but not so bad as Juris."

"Does he know who attacked them?"

"I am not knowing this. You should ask him, yes?"

"Yes, I think I will, Mr Balodis. Was Andris upset about the attack?"

"Yes, of course. His brother was in coma. He was very angry."

"Did he know who attacked Juris?"

Edgars paused, rubbing his chin, looking weary.

"I am not knowing this."

"And you can't think of anyone who would hold a grudge against either of your boys, any enemies they might have?"

"No, they are good boys, they work hard, go to university. Juris will be doctor."

"Ok, that's fine. Can you tell me when you last saw Andris?"

"It was at the hospital. Maybe last Wednesday."

"And when did you become concerned about him?"

Edgar's weariness was like a weight around his neck, dragging his head down onto his chest.

"When he's not home last night again and no message or word. Not answering phone to his mother. He is grown man now detective. I am not telling him where to be and what to do any more."

"No, I appreciate that, sir. I wasn't insinuating anything, just trying to get a time line in place. That'll be all for now. Just one more thing, can you give me a contact number or address for this Pete, please? What's his surname by the way?"

"Reynolds."

"Thanks, I think we better have a wee word with him."

"Yes, no problem."

After seeing Edgars Balodis out, Stark went to see Ian Barr, writing up notes on his computer, swearing like a trooper with every fouled keystroke.

"Ian, I need you to go and talk to this lad, Pete Reynolds. He was attacked along with the Balodis boy last week. See if he'll tell you who did it. After that, go and talk to the landlord at the Cross Words, check out if he knows anything about this assault that took place on his property."

"Aye, ok sir. Should I take a PC with me?"

The chance to abandon his keyboard based ineptitude restored Barr's usual enthusiasm for the job.

"Aye, if the Duty Sergeant is willing to spare one."

"Right, and what are you up to next then, sir?"

"I'm going to see if Archie Brown has any news for me. I'm no' a hundred per cent yet, but it seems pretty likely there's a link between the attack on Juris Balodis and the disappearance of his brother. See if you can get this Pete Reynolds character to give you some gen on them, find out if they had any enemies, that sort of thing."

"Right you are, sir. I'll get onto that the now. You got the guy's details?"

"Aye, here you go. Fill me in as soon as you get back."

Barr waved his agreement as he marched off to see the Duty Sergeant.

25. MUM'S THE WORD

"Stop here, Malky," said Billy.

Malky brought the car to a halt and Billy got out. "Wait a minute, I'll be back the now."

Billy jogged off, lumbering like a cart horse, this form of motion clearly adopted far too infrequently in recent years.

"Where's he away to?" asked Cammy.

Malky just shrugged.

After ten minutes, Billy returned, flushed and out of breath.

"Ok, let's go."

"Where were you off to, Da?"

"Never mind, eh. What the eye doesn't see, the heart can't grieve over."

"What?"

"I'm saying it's none of your business, ok. Come on Malky, let's go."

Mo was like the proverbial porker in manure – assuming said pig was a bit too keen on alcohol and didn't usually eat enough to maintain a decent body weight, of course.

"I could get used to this, Stella, eh."

Stella smiled as Mo glugged at her glass of wine, the gourmet burger and chips on her plate looking like a family of mice crept in and nibbled their fill when she wasn't looking. William shook his head, Mo oblivious to his scorn.

"What time did that wee shite say he was bringing the car back at?" asked William.

"Should be about ten minutes if he's on time. Just relax, son, he'll bring it back. Do you want anything else?"

"No, I'm fine thanks, Mum. That was lovely."

Stella smiled. A vision of the future she could look forward to. Time spent with her son and her sister, relaxing, not a care in the world. Then a hammer blow of realisation crashed into her gut. Jack. Here she was, living it up, drinking wine at two o'clock in the afternoon, while the wee mite was God knows where, enduring God knew what. She took out her phone; still no calls from Adam Stark or that other one, McGhee.

As she stared at the blank screen, a text popped up.

"That's Cammy in the car park. You two sit there, I'll go an' get the keys, eh."

"I better come with you," said William, pushing back his chair and making to stand.

"No. I don't want any fighting an' shouting. I've got enough on my plate with wee Jack. I don't need any more grief. Just stay here, I'll only be a few minutes."

"Mum, I won't let you go down there on your own. What about the you-know-what?" The proximity of other diner's made discretion necessary.

"No, that's fine, son. It's no' real, it's a fake, eh."

"Is that what he said?"

"Aye, he told me it was just a joke."

William refused to back down.

"Ok, maybe, but we've only got that lying little sod's word for that. I don't trust him. I'm coming with you and that's final."

"Ok, ok. But, I don't want any bloody nonsense between you pair. You can come along but let me talk to him."

"I'll be as good as gold, Mum. Promise."

Mo topped up her glass from the bottle sitting on the

table. "On you go, Stella. I'll wait here for you, hen. See youse in a minute."

Stella walked off. At the top of the stairs leading to the car park, she stopped and took some money out of the hole in the wall. Cammy was a pain in the arse but he was her pain in the arse and she could afford to be generous. After years of poverty and hardship, it was genuinely thrilling to visit cash machines without trepidation or pass them by in resignation. Now, they were like the magic porridge pot, and she loved her porridge.

With it being a weekday and not a holiday, the car park was quiet. Cammy got out of William's black BMW and stood in front of it. Stella waved and walked over to meet her son.

"Hi, Cammy, it's good to see you son, how are you doing?"

"I'm alright, Ma."

She hugged him but he didn't reciprocate. This was normal. He was a teenager after all.

He looked at William.

"There's your car back you wank."

"That's enough, Cammy. No bother wi' the polis then?"

William was puzzled. "Why's the boot open?" He walked around to close it.

Something made Stella shiver, a noise close by, she turned.

"Hello, Stella."

"Billy...Cammy, what the hell?"

Malky clattered William around the side of the head with the gun, causing him to fall into the boot, which he promptly slammed shut.

"William!"

"In the back, bitch."

Billy grabbed Stella by the arm and shoved her into the back of the car. Stella did as she was told, too shocked to react in any other way.

The engine fired up and they were heading out of the car park.

***

Barr, Stark and McGhee were gathered in the briefing room.

"Right Ian, tell Jim what you've just told me."

"Ok, sir. I went to talk to that lad Pete Reynolds first but couldn't get him on the phone, so on the way to his house I stopped at the Cross Words, eh."

"Bit early for a drink was it no' Barr? And you on duty too," quipped McGhee.

"Aye, very good, sir. The landlord was very defensive, looked like shit actually. I don't think he's got a high opinion of the polis. Anyhow, he claims to know nothing about the assault on Juris Balodis and Pete Reynolds."

"Did you believe him then?" asked McGhee.

"No' really, sir. But once I'd spoken to that Pete Reynolds, it was pretty clear he was lying."

Barr was flicking the pages of his notebook over as he spoke. The young man's meticulous nature impressed Stark. His typing skills may not have been honed but he had very neat handwriting by the look of it. Good to see he wasn't all jocularity and nonchalance.

"I went to see the lad Reynolds, still couldn't raise him by phone, so just rolled up at his door. He was in bed, feeling rough after a heavy night. At first, he wasn't going to talk to me about the attack, said he never saw who did it, it was a waste of our time, blah, blah, blah. But, when I told him we'd found a body, an' that we thought it might be Andris Balodis, he cracked like an egg, eh."

"Right then Barr, that's great, now cut to the chase, what did he tell you?"

"Turns out the attack was carried out by Malky McDuff."

"Jesus Christ! Really? He's definite about that?"

"Aye, a hundred per cent, sir. He was shitting himself, eh. Terrified of McDuff, well both of them actually. But, here's the best bit, sir. He says Andris Balodis threatened to get revenge on Malky for the attack. Said he was raging about his brother getting battered and promised Malky would be getting seen to."

McGhee went quiet. Frown deep enough to rest a book on, mouth hanging open. After a few seconds, he snapped out of his trance.

"Holy shit, this is unreal. Was Balodis no' scared of Malky then?"

"Naw, apparently, he's into martial arts, more than a bit handy according to Reynolds. But, he was still worried about him - told him Malky was a psycho an' so was Billy - but Balodis wouldn't listen."

"Jim, I'm sure you've joined the dots just like I have. Looks like Balodis went after Malky, as he promised he would, but came off second best. I don't think we can separate these cases quite so neatly now," said Stark.

The older man clasped his hands on top of his head.

"No, I don't think we can, Adam. Are we sure the body is definitely Andris Balodis yet?"

"I'm just waiting to hear from Archie Brown about going up to the mortuary with the Dad. I'm willing to put a few quid on it being him though."

"Aye, I don't think that's a wager I'll take you up on," said McGhee. "And what about the attack on Juris Balodis, what was the motive for that? Did Reynolds know?"

"Racist. Reynolds says Malky hates anyone from Eastern Europe. Well, he hates everyone and anyone that's no' a useless Scottish wanker like him, eh."

"Yes indeed, that man is a Grade A scumbag. Good work, Barr. You go an' get that lot typed up."

"Thanks, sir. I'll have a copy on your desk in about half an hour."

Stark wondered about such an ambitious timescale but

didn't say anything.

"Cheers. I need to brief the DCI and the Chief. As soon as we know that's Andris Balodis we found in the woods, bring Malky McDuff in, Adam."

"Aye, but if you remember, Jim. There were two sets of footprints at the scene."

"Oh, aye, so there were."

"And, who do you think Malky McDuff would turn to in his hour of need, disposing of a body?"

"Billy!"

"Yep, I'd put even more money on that."

"Right, get a rocket up that Archie Brown, take Balodis' father up there as soon as, an' let's get McDumb and McDumber in here for questioning."

26. ON THE ROAD AGAIN

Jack sat on the mattress, eyeing the bucket with suspicion and disgust. Hunger grumbled in his belly thanks to the meagre and erratic nature of the rations his captor provided. The latest inadequate batch of sustenance consisted of two packets of crisps, a can of coke and a chocolate bar. He stank, the room stank and he was exhausted. Sleep always fleeting, disturbed by dark thoughts and anxiety about what might happen next. Dreams full of shadows and dread whenever he did fall properly asleep.

He wanted a bath, he wanted to eat, he wanted to sleep in his own bed. He wanted to see his Mum.

All fire and fight evaporated after the shitfest of his last failed attempt at a jailbreak. The kidnapper's insistence that his parents had money, the kind of money worth holding him against his will to obtain, still baffled him.

Something else ate away at Jack. That voice. During the dung-hurling and struggle, an oral mask slipped, just for a moment. Something clicked, but he couldn't be right, didn't want to be right. A terrifying possibility. But, no matter how he tried to push it away, crushing realisation slowly overwhelmed him. Every time he heard a noise at the door, thought his jailer was coming back, panic ran a clawed finger up his spine.

He knew who it was and he could not be more scared.

***

"Jim, I've just been up to the mortuary with Edgars Balodis. The body in the woods was his laddie Andris right enough."

Stark was on his mobile, hands-free, driving back to the station having dropped the shattered Latvian off at his house.

"Ok, I'll start to gather a team together to go and pick up the McDuffs. What was the cause of death by the way?"

"Massive head injury. Archie reckons something very heavy but he's not ruled out hitting a kerb or something like that. Apparently, the laddie had a congenitally weak skull, any big bang on the head could have killed him."

"I thought he was into some kind of hardcore, ninja shit?"

"Aye, Archie said he was incredibly lucky not to have suffered any major problems before now. It was a time-bomb waiting to go off. The other injuries, like missing teeth and fingers were inflicted post mortem."

Stark swerved to avoid a cyclist, almost running into an oncoming van, horn blaring in protest as they slid past each other by the slimmest of margins.

"What was that?"

"Nothing mate, just driving back and some eejit got a bit too close."

"So, when did he reckon Balodis died?"

"Archie reckoned sometime late last Thursday or very early hours Friday."

"Right, that's all good. You can take the lead on this once you do get here. I'll see you back here in about fifteen minutes will I?"

"That sounds about right, Jim. Cheers."

Stark cancelled the call via the button on the steering wheel and hit the pedal hard, haunted by Edgars Balodis' face, crumpling as the cover was pulled back on his son. A proud man, a good man who worked hard, tried to do the best by his family, with his heart torn out.

As he drove, taking risks he'd normally vehemently admonish others for, he felt the familiar burning in his gut, remembering his own visit to identify Carrie because his Ma was too distraught. This time though, the flames of his guilt were being outrun to his head by a stifling fear about Mary.

Stark fired on some System Of A Down, ramped up the volume. Nothing like B.Y.O.B. to blow away the cobwebs, get the blood flowing freely. Stark was going to enjoy putting the McDuffs away. Those two had inflicted way more than their fair share of misery over the years. It was time for it to stop.

***

"Where are we going?" asked Stella.

"To the bank, to get my fuckin money," snarled Billy.

"What the fuck is wrong with you, Billy? I need the money for the ransom, eh."

"You leave me to worry about that, bitch. I want the money I'm due an' then, when I've got it, I'll find this fuckin kidnapper an' they'll be getting fuck all money."

"What are you on about, Billy? If you don't pay them, they'll hurt wee Jack."

"The only hurting going on will be me tearing that scum limb from limb."

"And what about William? Your arsehole brother just battered your eldest son round the head an' locked him in the boot of a car, an' you just let him do it. What kind of father are you?"

"That's no fuckin son of mine. He should have kept his faggot arse down in London where I didn't have to look at it. He makes me sick, so don't think I'll be worried if Malky decides to give him a wee bit more of that medicine, eh."

Stella's disgust threatened to rise up out of her stomach. How could she ever have let this repulsive excuse for a man touch her? She turned to Cammy, drilling a look towards him that he avoided by staring out the window.

"You got nothing to say for yourself, Cammy? Tricking me like that. After I gave you all that money as well. Looks like William was right, you are an ungrateful wee shite."

She'd pressed a button.

"As if I care what that bender thinks. Anyway, you're the one who ran off wi' all that money, left us to it. You've only got yourself to blame, Ma."

Stella sneered and shook her head in disgust.

"Malky, pull the car over now, before I call the cops an' get you all flung in jail."

She pulled out her mobile, but before she could even press a button, Billy reached round, grabbed it from her, opened his window and chucked it out.

"What was that you were saying, bitch? Don't you start issuing fuckin threats or I'll knock you're fuckin head off."

Stella began to feel properly scared but needed to stay cool. She didn't trust Malky's quiet brooding, that was not good.

"You haven't thought this through, Billy. How am I supposed to get you the money? You don't even have a bank account. I can't just walk into a bank an' ask them for millions in cash. They'll tell me to piss off, eh."

Billy was knocked off his stride, the elation at outflanking Stella in the car park blinded him to the fact that this new plan was badly thought through. Just like everything else in his life, he'd ballsed it up by failing to think ahead, clouded his judgement with anger and hubris.

"Aye, but I've got a bank account, Stella. Put your money in there an' then we'll sort Billy out after, eh."

Malky's suggestion was a great piece of improvisation in the face of their planning ineptitude.

"Aye, there you go. That's exactly what we'll do."

Stella battled to control her emotions.

"And say I won't do it? You can't force me, I'll tell the bank what you're up to an' they'll get the polis for me."

Malky skidded to a halt and turned round to face Stella.

"You'll do as your fuckin told, Stella, otherwise, that dunt round the head I gave precious wee William back there, will look like a tickle. Do you ken what I mean?"

Stella knew only too well what Malky meant. She'd seen him dish out a few beatings in her time and she wouldn't be letting him loose on William if she could help it.

"Ok, let's get this over with. Take me to the bank."

***

"Right guys, let's be clear about this. Both McDuff brothers are unpredictable and potentially violent. We don't need any heroes ending up in the hospital or on a slab. If you find either of them, you call it in and wait for back-up. Is that clear?"

The gathering gave various indications of understanding Stark but he knew it guaranteed nothing as far as a clean, painless result went.

"Ok, that's good, now let's get out there and get this pair gathered up with the minimum amount of fuss."

The teams streamed out of the briefing room, leaving Stark and McGhee on their own.

"Let's hope nobody decides to be a hero, Jim."

"Aye. Listen, Adam, we mustn't lose sight of the fact that a nine year old is still missing. I'm really concerned that we've no' heard anything else from the kidnapper. So far, we've drawn a blank from all the CCTV and door-to-door. I might haul Greg Marshall over the coals again. He's our best bet so far and I'm not convinced he was telling the whole truth."

"I know, I was thinking about Jack earlier as well. I agree with giving Marshall another going over. I still don't think he's got the bottle but stranger things have happened."

Stark and McGhee started walking.

"Incidentally, did you ever track down Connelly, the paedo that had his house burned down?" asked Stark.

"Aye, it turns out he bought a caravan out near Perth somewhere. His probation officer has vouched for him, says he's been keeping his nose clean, turning up for therapy sessions, doing all the stuff his bail requires of him."

"Hmm. That kind of blows Billy McDuff's theory out the water then."

"Aye, it would certainly seem that way. I've decided to run up to Perth later and have a word anyway. No harm in marking his card, seeing how he reacts face-to-face."

"Good idea, need to rule him out, even if he seems an unlikely candidate."

Stark put his jacket on.

"Right, Ian, you finished that report yet?"

"Aye, just about to put it on DI McGhee's desk the now, sir."

"Good, you're with me. Let's go an' see if we can find the McDuffs."

After turning up nothing at any of the three McDuff households, getting no answer from any of their phones, drawing a blank at the pub, and finding out from the hotel the women were using that they'd been out since mid-morning, Stark, Barr and the three other teams reconvened in the police station car park.

"Right, has anybody thought of any other obvious places to check where we haven't looked yet?" asked Stark.

There were murmurs and a general consensus, by shrug and shaken head, that they didn't have any more to offer. Stark was annoyed and frustrated.

"Ok, team one, go to Billy's house and team two go to Malky's. Team three, I want you to take the Cross Words. Me and DC Barr will take the hotel. It looks like we'll need to sit this out, wait for them to break cover."

Stark felt his phone vibrate.

"DI Stark."

"Sir, I've got Maureen Watson on the line. She wants to speak to you or DI McGhee, says it's urgent."

"I'm out in the car park Anne, I'll come in and take it on the land line."

"Ok, sir."

"Listen up guys, don't move on that order just yet. I have a call to take, which might change things. Give me a minute."

He walked into the building, heading straight to the switchboard. Anne Cameron handed him a headset.

"I should warn you, sir. She sounds a bit worse for drink."

"Ok Anne, thanks."

"Maureen, it's DI Stark here. How can I help you?"

"Listen, it's Billy, he's taken Stella an' William, I'm sure he has. She went to get the car, an' she's no' come back an' William went but he's no' come back either, eh."

"Maureen, slow down. Take this one step at a time. What do you mean Billy has taken Stella an' William?"

"I told you, she went to get the car."

"What car, Maureen?"

"William's car, that Cammy nicked, borrowed, took."

"Cammy stole William's car?"

"Aye, naw, em, he borrowed it without his permission – for a joke, eh. Anyway, she went to get it back an' she's disappeared. An' so has William."

"Where did this happen, Maureen?"

"Stirling, Thistle Centre, earlier on."

"What makes you think Billy's taken them?"

"I tried phoning her but she's no' answering, she wouldn't just fuck off without so much as a cheerio. It's him, I know it."

"Ok Maureen, but she did abscond earlier in the month without leaving word."

"That was totally fuckin different. I should have known

you wouldn't help me. I should have spoken to that other guy, what is it...McGhee."

"I will help you Maureen. Now, tell me, what kind of car was it?"

"A big black one. Fancy. BMW I think. William's no' short of a bob or two, you ken."

"I don't suppose you know the registration?"

"How the fuck would I ken that?"

"Alright, that's fine, just try to keep calm. I'm trying to help you here."

The slurring and incoherence of drink were all too evident in Mo's speech and if they didn't need a break so badly, Stark would likely have dismissed this as nonsense; with nothing better to go on, he stuck with it.

"We can look the registration up on the computer. When exactly did Stella and William go missing?"

"I'm no' sure, eh. About three maybe or two. After lunch anyway."

Stark looked at his watch – depending on which of Mo's times was right - they had been gone up to two hours.

"Ok Maureen. Where are you the now?"

"Me? I'm still in the Thistle Centre."

"Right, you stay there. I'll call you if I find Stella, ok?"

"Ok, but get on wi' it, that Billy's a bad bastard when his temper's up. I dread to think what he might do to Stella."

"Right you are, Maureen. I'll call you if I get any news, bye."

Once he'd hung up, Stark got onto the computer. After a bit of messing about trying to nail down the registration, he finally came up trumps. Next stop was a torturous encounter with McLaren, who was as awkward as possible before agreeing to smooth over any jurisdiction issues relating to the teams going into Stirling.

With the necessary permissions underway, Stark made his way back out to the car park and gathered the teams around again.

"Right, this is likely a wild goose chase but Maureen Watson says Billy McDuff has abducted his wife Stella and his eldest son William from the Thistle Centre in Stirling. I have the car registration, which we'll also put into the ANPR. It's a black BMW 525i.

"I don't have any gen on where they might have gone after leaving the Centre but I'm going to get the Centre security team to run the tapes from their cameras and see what they can come up with. DC Barr, you an' me are going over there now to check that out. The rest of you head out to the points we agreed before. If we get a fix on them, I'll let you know."

The teams dispersed. Stark and Barr got into their car, Barr driving.

"Right Ian, get the lights and sirens on. We need to get to Stirling quick smart. I have a feeling Maureen might be right, and if she is, then Stella McDuff could be in big trouble."

27. BANK ON IT

Stella was shaking, mouth sticky dry, skin clammy. The bank, quiet, only a couple of other customers in there with her, tellers going about their business as if this was just any other day.

She approached the counter and spoke to the girl behind the partition. Helen, her name badge said, pretty, sixteen or seventeen by the look of her, corporate rictus firmly set.

"Hi, hen. I need to transfer some money, eh."

"Ok, madam, how much would you like to transfer?"

"Two million quid."

The young girl frowned then burst out laughing.

"Sorry, madam, did you just say two million pounds?"

The other two customers' interest was instantly piqued, Stella flushed scarlet. Anger rising as well as embarrassment.

"Don't you bloody laugh at me, hen. I know what I said, now can you just do as I asked, eh."

The girl realised Stella was being serious and her own skin reddened.

"I, I'm sorry. I can't authorise that kind of money. I'll need to speak to my manager."

"Aye, ok, but hurry up will you?"

Stella turned away from the counter back into the foyer.

"What the fuck are you two gawping at?"

Both gawpers made a hasty exit.

After a couple of minutes, a tall, authoritative woman came through from a doorway to Stella's right.

"Hello, I'm Madeline Short, I'm the branch manager, I understand you'd like to undertake a sizeable transaction, Mrs...?"

She stuck out her hand for Stella to shake.

"McDuff, Stella McDuff."

"Ok, Mrs McDuff, can I ask you to come with me to a more private area, where we can sort this out for you?"

"Aye, fine."

Once parked on the luxurious, black leather settee in the ante room, Stella began to relax slightly.

"Tea? Coffee?" offered Ms Short.

"Em, naw, I'm fine, thanks."

"Ok, so my colleague, Helen, informs me that you'd like to transfer two million pounds. Is that right?"

"Aye, an' before you start, I won the lottery, six and a half million, so I've got the cash. I'm no' ripping the piss here."

The bluntness threw the bank manager a little.

"Oh, right, I see. Well, that's fine, I'm sorry if Helen was a little unsure, we don't get that many people like you in here. Congratulations by the way. I've never actually met a real-life winner, a millionaire. What's it like winning so much?"

"It was great, now, never mind all that. I don't have time for chatting. Can you just move my money for me an' I can get on my way?"

Madeline Short wasn't too enamoured by Stella's attitude and manner. She decided not to be as helpful as she might have been if Stella had seen fit to be a little more polite, friendly.

"Well, the thing is, we can't just authorise this sort of money transfer without some security checks. Can you please provide me with two forms of identification, one of which needs to be photographic and another which has your current address on it."

"What? Are you taking the piss? It's my money, an' if I want to transfer it I bloody well will. Here's my bank card, an' there's my card for the social. That should be plenty, eh."

"Mrs McDuff, please don't swear at me. I'm only doing my job. I'll very gladly make the transaction but I cannot do it without the security checks. You must produce a recent utility bill, telephone bill or something similar that shows your name and address on it. The system is there to protect you against fraud and theft and I cannot circumvent it."

"Circumwhat it?"

"I can't go around it, I must follow the procedure as stated in the policies laid down by the bank."

Stella could feel the world shutting down around her. If she didn't get this money transferred, William would be beaten to a pulp, or maybe worse. Her beautiful, beautiful boy. And what about Jack, who had Jack, how would she get him back? Shadows crept into the corners of her vision, she could hear blood screaming in her ears, a cacophony of colours, sounds and smells whirled through her head. She couldn't breathe. The tall woman sitting opposite her was talking but the words were slowing down, distorted, scrambled. Everything folded away in a great rush of air and colour, then darkness engulfed her.

***

The control room in the shopping centre wasn't really designed to have so many people in it at one time. Barely able to stand shoulder to shoulder, unwelcome and inappropriate intimacy a strong possibility with any sudden movement.

"Right, so that's the car coming in," said Dave the camera operator, "and that's them parking up."

Two figures emerged from the car. Stark recognised

them. The McDuff brothers positioned themselves back in the shadows, behind pillars holding up the layers of concrete parking cake.

"Now, here comes the woman and another guy."

They all watched dumbfounded as the events played out in front of them.

"Holy crap, sir. Maureen was right."

"Aye, she was, Ian. Have we got the car leaving the building, Dave?"

"Just a second, yes, here we go. They stopped briefly to pay for their ticket and crossed the barrier at 14.50."

"Just to confirm, Dave, they have to turn left out of here do they?"

"Yes, it's a no right turn as they exit. Two lanes though. Outside one means you can turn right up towards Wellgreen or go onto Craigs roundabout. Inside one takes you to Craigs roundabout but means you're taking first exit to left."

"Can we see which lane they took?"

"Not with our cameras but I think the council ones might have caught them. To be honest though, I don't know how much good it'll do you, there's a ton of options once they hit that roundabout. I don't think knowing which lane they took will resolve where they went next."

"No, probably not. Ok, well, we can follow that up if we have to. Can I have a copy of that?"

"Aye, give me a minute an' I'll burn you a copy. It's all DVD these days."

"Thanks Dave, you've been incredibly helpful."

The two cops got back in their car, Stark phoning McGhee and McLaren to update them.

"What now, sir?"asked Barr once Stark finished his calls.

"We get an APB out on that car an' we make sure we get to them before something bad happens to Stella."

***

"Mrs McDuff? Mrs McDuff, can you hear me?"

Stella could feel the world returning to meet her, light danced again and the screaming in her ears had gone, replaced by a dull thud in her temples.

Madeline Short was patting Stella's hand and talking softly, all her indignation chased away by the shock at Stella's sudden loss of consciousness.

"Hello, Mrs McDuff. How are you feeling?"

"Not so good, hen. Can I have a wee drink of water, please?"

"Of course. Helen, can you fetch Mrs McDuff a glass of water, thank you."

The younger girl went off for a few seconds before returning with a glass. Stella sipped, the cooling sensation bringing her thoughts back into sharp, terrifying focus.

"How's that? Better?" asked Madeline.

"Aye, that's good, thanks. Listen, I need your help, hen."

The bank manager sat back on her own chair again.

"Go on, what can I do for you."

"I *have* to get that money transferred, eh. It's a matter of life an' death."

"Mrs McDuff, are you being blackmailed or coerced into handing over your money?" Madeline had been on some special courses, ones to help prepare branch managers for all sorts of unusual situations that most of them would never face in a thirty year career. She was facing one now.

Stella hesitated, trying to compose herself; trapped, hemmed in by choices; all leading toward disaster for someone she cared about. A tear cut a path through her foundation, taking a black streak of mascara with it as it descended.

"I, I, my son William's in danger if I don't get them this money. Please, I'm begging you, please help me."

Madeline knew the procedure, it was time to involve the police but she needed to get some details.

"Ok, Mrs McDuff, who wants this money from you?"

"Please, you don't understand, they'll hurt William really badly. Please."

"Who is they, Mrs McDuff?"

"My husband and his brother."

That was not the answer Madeline had been expecting. She felt physically sick, how could this be? She needed to stay calm, follow the procedure, get as much information as she could, save judgement and disgust for later.

"Oh my word, that's terrible. Where are they now?"

"They're outside in the car. They're waiting for me to go back an' tell them it's all ok. If I don't, they'll hurt him."

Stella was sobbing freely now. Madeline gave her a box of tissues from the table.

"Mrs McDuff, you'll not like this, but I must involve the police. This is really serious and I cannot, under any circumstances, authorise a transfer under these conditions."

"No!" screeched Stella. "Have you no' listened to a fuckin word I've told you. They'll hurt him if I go to the polis, you can't tell them, you just can't! William, they'll fuckin kill him. Please, please, please, no polis."

Madeline stood up.

"I'm so sorry Mrs McDuff, this must be awful for you but I have to do what I've been trained to do. Please stay here while I place a call to the police. I'll send Helen in to sit with you."

Stella exploded out of her chair, pushed Madeline out of the way and bolted for the door. Madeline reeled, stumbled and fell back as Stella ran for the main exit.

Out in the street, she ran to the car, pulled open the door, sat down in the back.

"Malky, get the fuck out of here now! The polis are on their way."

"What the fuck have you done, bitch? Have you

transferred the money?" shouted Malky.

"They wouldn't let me. I told you they wouldn't but you wouldn't listen to me, would you, Malky. Drive you idiot, before the polis get here!"

Malky turned the engine over and they roared off.

28. WHAT YOU WANT

Stark and Barr came to a stop outside the bank and charged inside, leaving car doors open, blocking the street.

"Are they still here?" shouted Stark as soon as he got into the foyer.

"No, you've missed them. Mrs McDuff bolted about twenty minutes ago."

"Bollocks! Did anybody see which way they went?"

The bank manager crossed the foyer and extended her hand. "Madeline Short, I'm the manager here."

Stark's spell was broken by this striking woman. Tall, curvy, immaculately dressed, dark-framed glasses that matched her raven black hair. He took her hand, feeling a surge of energy course up his arm.

"Detective Inspector Adam Stark," he said, pulling out his warrant card. "Sorry about the language, on a bit of a mission. Did anyone see which way they went after she left?"

"Helen? Can you tell the Detective Inspector what you saw, please."

The young teller stepped forward, blushing and avoiding eye contact. "Mrs McDuff ran out the door, crossed over the street and got into a black car. I'm not very good with cars but it looked expensive. They sat there for a few seconds then drove off up the street."

"Anything else you can tell me, Helen?"

"Well, I stepped out into the street, took a note of the

registration. I can get you that if you want it?"

"Yes, that's great, thanks. At the top there, which way did they turn?"

"Em, I think it's a one way, they can only go right."

Stark felt slightly foolish, he knew that, but was so focussed on the chase, he'd forgotten what the road layout was like in the middle of Alloa these days.

"Of course. Right, DC Barr, let's get on the road. They've got a head start but they can't have gotten too far. Mrs Short, I'll send someone round to take a statement from you."

"Actually, Detective Inspector, it's Ms Short."

Stark could sense a crackle of electricity fly between them. "Oh, sorry, right you are. In the meantime, here's my card. Call me if you think of anything that might be relevant, no matter how small."

He took her hand again and their gaze lingered that little bit longer than normal.

"Ok, Detective Inspector, I'll do that."

Back in the car, Stark made calls to McGhee and McLaren again. They needed to regroup. All the traffic units in Central Scotland were on alert for the BMW, it was pointless them just charging about without a plan of action, hoping to bump into them by chance.

"She was a bit of a looker sir, eh," said Barr.

"What, who, the bank manager?"

"Aye, that's right sir, *Ms* Short, the one you were slavering over back there, hahaha!"

"Listen, Barr, she was the one slavering. And, let's be honest, can you blame her?"

"Aye, right enough, sir. If I wasn't married I reckon I might do you."

"In your fuckin dreams, pal!"

***

The car had been sitting still for a few minutes, a dark, uneasy atmosphere cloaking the occupants.

"What are we going to do now, Billy?" asked Malky.

"I don't know, Malky. Fuck's sake."

Stella jumped as the banging from the boot started up.

"Oh great, that's gayboy awake then," said Cammy.

"Billy, you need to stop this now. I'll get you some money, just let me an' William go."

"What, you reckon I believe that do you? As soon as I let you go, you're going straight to the polis, eh."

"No, I swear, I'll get you some money. Fuck the polis, I don't need them to sort this out. The only thing I want is a divorce. You can keep the laddies wi' you, an' we'll go our separate ways. What do you say?"

Billy rubbed his face vigorously with both hands.

"How can I trust you, Stella? You won that money an' your first thought was to fuck off an' leave me wi' nowt."

"Aye, that was wrong, Billy. I know that, I've been feeling bad. I gave you some money already but I would have seen you right. I still can, eh. I understand you're angry, if you'd done that to me, I'd have been angry too. I don't care about all of this, just stop now, before it gets too serious. We can sort out the money."

Malky decided it was time to intervene.

"Billy, this lying bitch will fuck us over. You do know that, eh? Anyway, we're already in bother, we need money, an' we need to get the fuck out of Alloa as soon as we can."

Billy's head was turning thoughts over like a croupier on speed. The banging from the back was incessant.

Suddenly, Malky got out and walked round to the rear of the car. Stella panicked, scrambling out after him. Cammy and Billy followed suit. Malky yanked open the boot and dragged William out.

"What the fuck?"

"Shut your fuckin mouth, faggot!"

Malky took the gun and pushed it against William's

head. Stella screamed and tried to rush him, but Billy grabbed her, holding her back as she thrashed, delivering a slap that drained all her resistance.

"Uncle Malky, please, what the hell's going on?"

"I told you not to talk, you freak. Your Ma here owes me some money, an' unless I get it, I'm going to blow your fuckin bender brains out."

"Malky, please, I told you I'll get Billy the money. I just can't get it today, the bank has security they won't change. I need to have the right stuff wi' me, like id an' that. They won't do it without it," pleaded Stella.

"I don't give a fuck how you do it, you get me that money today, bitch."

Cammy didn't like this. Things were getting out of hand. William acted like a dickhead sometimes, it disgusted him that he fucked other men, but he didn't want his uncle to actually shoot him. William hadn't done anything wrong. He didn't take the money and fuck off, Stella did. Even so, she was still his Mum, he wouldn't want anything really bad to happen to her either.

"Uncle Malky, come on, that's enough, you've made your point. Just lock him back in the boot an' let's find a bank that'll pay up, eh."

"Cammy's right, Malky. Please stop, this is getting crazy. I told you I'll get you the money. Billy, please this is your son. And what about Jack, have you forgotten about him?" Stella pleaded.

Malky had gone to that place of rage which spelt danger in big neon capital letters.

"Fuck you Stella, and your bastard kids. I need money and if I don't get it, you won't be seeing this gay fuck or that wee shite Jack, ever again. Get me my fuckin money!"

Billy looked at his brother quizzically, the wildness in Malky's eyes beyond anything he'd seen before. A recklessness even Billy found disturbing.

"What the fuck are you talking about, Malky?"

Malky stood up. William scurried backwards, trying to

regain his feet, get away from the madman sticking a gun in his face, threatening to kill him.

"You're a fuckin prick Billy, you always have been. I knew you wouldn't give me what I was due. I needed a wee insurance policy, eh."

Billy and Stella looked at each other, the enormity of what Malky seemed to be saying, swelling like a giant balloon in front of them.

"And as for you, Stella, you've always hated me, always sided with that slag of a sister of yours. I wasn't going to get a fuckin penny from you unless I took things into my own hands.

"So, here's how it's going to go down. I'm taking the car, an' me an' Stella are going for a wee ride. Tomorrow, she's going to get me my money, then I'm going to disappear. Once I'm safely out of the country, I'll tell you where wee Jack is."

Billy felt the ground swim in front of him. He struggled to keep his focus. The foreground rushed away into the distance taking everything in his life with it.

"Oh, my, fuckin, god! You took Jack?" whispered Cammy.

Malky raised the gun, pointing it at Stella. "In the car. Now."

"Fuck you Malky, Cammy told me the gun's a fake. You better tell me what you did wi' Jack or it'll be you that's getting fuckin killed."

Stella heard a primal noise, guttural, strangled rage. Motion from beside her.

"No, Da, the gun's real. I lied to Ma!"

Too late. Billy collided with Malky, slamming into him like a furious steam engine. The two men fell to the ground, the gun went off, report ringing in the air before everything went still. Gunsmoke and disbelief twisted upward together as rain began to fall.

***

The night, full of sound and coloured lights. Paramedics, police and SOCO milling around the scene. Gathering evidence, clearing up the aftermath.

Stella sat on the back steps of an ambulance, wrapped in a blanket, William comforting her. Stark, Barr and McGhee walked across the muddy ground, rain dancing on puddles as they went.

"Hello, Stella," said McGhee.

"Aye, very good. You're too late. I asked you to help save my laddie. I said I would pay but now I can't, an' the only person who knew where he was is dead."

"What the hell happened?" asked Stark.

"Uncle fuckin Malky, that's what happened, Detective Stark," said William. "He was always a nutter but I never thought he would stoop so low as to kidnap his own nephew for money."

"It was Malky took Jack?"

"So he said, right before my Dad attacked him, and he ended up with a bullet in his chest."

McGhee exhaled heavily.

"Where's Billy now?"

"He's over there in that cop car." William pointed at a marked squad car about fifty metres away. "Took three of your lot to get him cuffed and stop him punching Malky's lifeless face to a pulp."

"Bloody hell. What a mess. So, you've got no clue where Malky might have been keeping the wee man?"

Stella shook her head, tears beginning to flow. "No, an' we never will now."

"Where did the gun come from, Stella?"

She looked at William, narrowing her eyes, sniffing.

"It was Malky's, I never knew he had a gun. Wasn't his usual style. Billy tried to get it off him, Malky shot himself by accident when Billy jumped on him."

William looked away to his left. Cammy was standing under an umbrella with a uniformed cop. He'd sort that little bastard out later; go along with his Ma covering for him...for now.

"Right, I see. Ok, look, you need to get a good night's rest. We'll get you all into the station tomorrow morning for statements. We've arrested Billy an' he'll be spending the night in the cells," said McGhee.

"What about Jack? Are you going to start looking for him?" asked William.

"I'll be going to speak with our boss in a minute. Decide how to go about looking for Jack. Now the ransom thing and any threats of violence are off the agenda, we can get on with a proper search. Don't worry, we'll find him, Stella. I'm sure we will."

Stark and Barr went across to speak to Billy, while McGhee spoke to the DCI and the Chief about setting up a press conference and organising a full-scale manhunt for the missing boy.

Stark knocked on the driver's window.

"DI Stark. Can I have a word with your prisoner, thanks."

"Aye, go ahead, sir."

Stark got into the back of the car alongside Billy, chin resting on his chest, eyes glazed over.

"Billy, I need to ask you one question before you go back to the station."

His head came up as if in slow motion, the glazed eyes re-igniting with fire at the sound of Stark's voice.

"You, can get yourself to fuck! I've got nothing to say to you, you prick!"

"Aye, fair enough Billy, but if you want us to find Jack, I need to ask you one thing. Where do you think Malky might have kept him?"

"I've got no fuckin idea, now fuck off an' leave me alone."

"No idea at all, Billy? Really? No-one knew him better than you. It could be a shed, a flat, a caravan. Think man. Your son's life could depend on it."

The fire in Billy's eyes dimmed a little.

"I can't think of anywhere. No."

"Ok, that's fine. We'll be starting a major search tomorrow. Let's hope we can find the wee man without your help."

Stark got into the passenger seat of McGhee's car. Time to gather thoughts, share a problem. Barr jumped in the back, glad to get out of the rain.

"Jim, there's something nagging at me about this situation."

"Oh aye, what's that?"

"How come nobody can come up with an obvious place where Malky would have held Jack captive?"

"Sorry, I don't get you. Why would it need to be obvious? Surely, for something like this the more secret the better?"

"Well, aye, but Malky's no' exactly loaded is he. He's no' going to have a second home – Barr searched his main flat in a matter of seconds. He wasn't a gardener, an' they've no grandpa or father wi' an allotment as far as I know. He's no' had a job for years, so he's no' got access to anywhere like a building site. For the life of me, I can't think where he could keep the laddie captive for days or weeks on end."

McGhee folded his arms across his chest and pondered.

"You think he's got a partner?"

"Maybe, aye. Someone who's provided the hideaway."

"Who though, sir?" asked Barr, who'd been listening intently to his boss's musings.

"I don't know. Again, it's no' obvious. I can't see it being one of the family but, after what's gone on so far, we can't totally rule that out."

"That Cammy seems a bit shifty to me, sir, " said Barr, "and there was a funny look went his way from his brother earlier."

"Aye, I saw that too, but I don't think it'll be anything to do wi' him. Again, he doesn't have money or access to somewhere to keep the wee man hidden."

"No, right enough, sir."

They all dropped into quiet contemplation for a few moments.

"Jim, did SOCO bag a mobile phone for Malky?"

"I would have thought so. Everyone's got one these days don't they – even unemployed wasters like Malky."

"I want to check out who he's been calling, an' who's been calling him, in the last week or so. If he's been getting help on this, we might just find them that way."

"That's a bloody good shout, Adam. I knew McLaren was an arse for trying to sideline you."

"Ian, quick, go and get that phone from SOCO before they pack up and go. We can spend a couple of hours checking out the numbers an' see where it leads us."

"Ok sir, will do."

29. CALL ME

Stark began reading out the numbers on the phone and Barr ticked off any of the ones they'd gathered from the family. McGhee sat at his desk, writing up a report and listening in at the same time.

There were a couple of calls to Billy and another to Cammy. Apart from that, there were only three numbers to check.

"Thank fuck he was a miserable wee shit, wi' next to no pals, sir."

"Aye, this should make our life a lot easier. What about texts? Any of them?" asked Stark.

"Em, no. Looks like he wasn't the most tech savvy guy. There's just one here to Billy, eh. Something a bit jumbled about meeting at the pub."

"Right, so let's see who answers the phone when we call them shall we?"

"Aye, on you go, sir."

Stark hit dial on the phone and listened to the first unknown number ring and ring and ring. Eventually, it went to a continuous tone, indicating the call had timed out.

"No-one home there then. Let's try this next one."

Again he hit dial and the phone at the other end began to ring.

"Alloa Taxi Hire."

"Sorry, wrong number," said Stark, cancelling the call.

"Who was that, sir?"

"Local taxi firm. Right, last one. Keep all your bits crossed."

Stark hit dial, the phone barely registered one ring before connecting.

"Hello, Malky? Thank fuck, I thought something had gone wrong. You there? Malky? Hello?"

Stark disconnected the call.

"Shit, that's our boy. I was right, he's got an accomplice."

McGhee shot out of his chair. "Fuckin hell, Adam. Call him back!"

"No, Jim. I've got a better idea."

Stark began to compose a text.

Sorry, got cut off. Need to meet. Outside Rugby Club in 20 mins. Malky.

"Ooh, you sneaky bugger, Adam. Where did you pick that one up from?"

"Aye, an old boss used it to nail a drug dealer once. Never thought I'd get the chance to do it as well, but there you go."

The phone beeped twice to indicate a response.

OK.

"Damn, he didn't sign off. Never mind, we've still got the bastard," said Stark.

"Right, action stations, let's get suited and booted. We've got a wee laddie to rescue. Adam, you take the lead on this. I'll let the big bosses know what's going on."

"Ok. If you're sure. Technically, you were looking after the kidnap thing. It's your collar by rights is it no'?"

"Look, Adam, I'm too long in the tooth for all that pish. It's your turf, you nailed him wi' the phone, you can nail him in person. Never mind standing here arguing, get

216

your arses down to that Rugby Club!"

30. CATCH AND RELEASE

The streetlight cast its inadequate glow on proceedings. No big issue as far as Stark was concerned. He and Barr parked opposite the Clubhouse, hunkered down in their seats. Another car positioned itself a little further on.

Spot on the twenty minute mark since sending his text, a Mercedes saloon pulled into the car park, killing it's lights as it stopped. The car faced away from the street so they couldn't see the driver. Stark lifted his radio.

"Go, go, go!"

The two cars raced into the car park, hemming the Merc in. Stark, Barr and two uniforms leapt from their vehicles. Stark pulled open the driver's door of the Merc, hauled the startled driver out and up against the side of his car.

"Police! You're under arrest!" shouted Stark cuffing the driver before turning him around to face them.

"Fuckin hell, sir. That's Jonny Jacobs, the landlord of the Cross Swords."

"What the hell's going on here, officer? There must be some sort of misunderstanding."

"I don't think so, mate."

Stark frisked him, locating his mobile phone in a trouser pocket. He brought it to life and pressed the messages icon. There, on the screen, was Stark's bogus text from the not-so-dearly departed Malky McDuff.

"Care to explain how that text got there then?"

"Oh, dear Christ, what have I done?"

"With luck, nothing too drastic. Do yourself a favour an' tell me where the boy is," said Stark.

"He's at the pub, in a basement room. He's fine. I, I'm sorry."

"It's no' me you need to apologise to, pal."

Stark read Jacobs his rights and they bundled him into the car. Stark got on the radio to McGhee.

"Jim, get someone round to the Cross Swords pub. The landlord, Jonny Jacobs, was the accomplice. The laddie's in a basement room."

"Fuck me. Ok, great work, Adam. I'm on it. I'll see you back at the nick. Cheers."

**

Stark sat down opposite Stella and William, exhaustion and trauma etched on their faces. He was drained himself.

"Thanks for coming in guys. How are you doing?"

"We're ok, thanks," said William. "Just a bit tired."

Stella looked close to tears. Suddenly, she stood, walked around the table and hugged Stark.

"Thank you."

"You're welcome."

She let go of him, returned to her seat.

"How is the wee man?"

"He's round at Maureen's, sleeping. Poor wee mite's been through hell. He needed a good feed, a bath and a decent bed. That bastard Jacobs didn't even try to look after him," said Stella. "He told me Malky came round a couple of times and, the second time, he guessed that's who it was. He remembered what happened to wee Tina. He was terrified. I've told him it's ok and Uncle Malky can't hurt him any more but it's going to take time, eh."

"Aye, I'm sure it'll be a wee while before he's totally right again."

"So, what the fuck was this guy Jacobs all about then,

Detective Stark?" asked William. "We've never even met the guy."

"Aye, well, you probably knew that Malky an' Billy were regulars in Jacobs' pub for years. They had a pretty spiky relationship at times but recently, Jacobs has been in severe financial bother. Malky knew this and took his chance to tempt him into getting some of your money to save the pub from going under."

"He tortured my wee laddie so he could keep his fuckin pub open?" spat Stella.

"Afraid so. No' exactly master criminals though. They left DNA and fingerprints all over the place. We even got a partial from Jacobs on the ransom note.

"It was just good old fashioned greed on Malky's part, an' desperation on Jacobs'. We intend to throw the book at him. He'll be going down for a long time for this."

William exhaled loudly and shook his head.

"So he fuckin should."

"Anyway, I thought you'd like to know this stuff. Help you get it straight in your head."

"Aye, thanks, it does help," said William.

They stood to leave and Stark gathered his notes. Stella stopped in the doorway and turned back.

"Adam. Is it ok if I call you Adam?"

"What? Aye. If you want."

"Anyway, Adam, I just wanted to say I'm sorry."

"What for?"

"For all the shitty things I said to you, for the way Billy an' Maureen an' Malky treated you. For no' believing you when you said you'd find Jack, eh."

Stark actually felt himself choke up. He looked at the floor, swallowing hard, desperate not to cry in front of Stella.

"Thanks again. If there's ever anything I can do for you, just ask."

"Ok Stella, thanks, and no worries, I was just doing my job."

She left. Shell-shocked, Stark stood there for a good two minutes before his legs started working again and he could find the energy to move.

31. DEATH AND LIFE

Hand shaking and accepting commiserations were beginning to grow a little wearisome. Stark felt his energy levels flicker.

Ian Barr sidled up to him, pint in hand, looking a bit worse for wear.

"Hi, sir, just wanted to say how sorry I am, eh."

"Again, Ian."

"Aye, right. Well, you've been a great boss to me, sir. I just wanted you to know that."

Stark laughed. Barr was quality company, a proper diamond and a great colleague. He looked across the room. Kirsty Barr was nibbling on a sausage roll, standard fare at any Scottish wake. Drinking an orange juice, less so.

"Oh, did I tell you, sir? You mind of what's his face, em, Greg Marshall? You know, the guy wi' the sick kid that sent that note to the McDuffs."

"Aye, poor bastard."

"Well, it turns out, Stella paid for the kid to go to America for that treatment he needed. That's pretty big of her do you no' think, sir."

"Aye, it sure is, Ian. Money can bring the good out in some folk I suppose."

"Aye," slurred Barr becoming unsteady on his feet. "Listen, sir. Can I ask you something?"

"Go on then, Ian. Fire away."

"What's the script wi' you an' the McDuffs? How come

Billy hates you so much?"

Stark shook his head.

"Ach, it goes way back to when we were teenagers. Stella was a bit of a looker back then you know."

"It's funny you should say that, sir. I actually thought she might have been fit in her day. Three kids, forty a day, a Scottish diet an' twenty odd years didn't do her any favours, but still."

"Aye, well, she was going out wi' Billy, but one night me an' her did the business. Billy found out, went mental, an' him an' Malky tried to batter me. I gave as good as I got, an' he never forgave me."

"Oh, you dirty dog, you!"

"Nah, it was a long time ago, Ian. We were just daft kids. It's ancient history, man."

"It's funny though, sir. Now you mention it. I did think that William had your eyes, eh."

"Fuck off Ian, you twat!"

They laughed like a couple of hyenas.

Stark surveyed the room. People he knew, people he didn't, from a wide range of ages. All of them there to say sorry and to let him know how much his Ma meant to them.

It was fine. Actually, it was more than fine. She'd have loved the day if she'd been there. The sun shone, relatives he barely remembered showed up from all over the world, it wasn't sad or sombre but respectful enough. He found it refreshing to go to a funeral free from religion. Mary was a humanist, abandoning God when he abandoned her and the ceremony was a celebration of her life, her achievements. There was no kowtowing or forelock tugging to some supreme supernatural being, no being thankful she was gone because she was in a better place. People laughed and cried, drank, told stories, drank, sang songs, drank and listened to some of her favourite music. Some of them just drank.

Stark was tired and sad but the terror he'd felt months

ago, when she told him her time was limited, had dissipated, retreated to somewhere less obvious. Losing her would leave a gaping chasm in his life. Visiting the graveside would be tougher than ever but, somehow, he felt less daunted by the prospect of being alone. Maybe it was the precious time they'd spent in the last couple of months; visiting Paris, riding a roller-coaster, swimming in the sea off Tiree. Memories to treasure, when looking forward might not bring such succour. Perhaps the terror would return but, for now, he'd enjoy its absence.

The being back in Alloa thing was still up for debate. He'd keep his options open there. McLaren was still being a bit of a dick, despite the result. Stark crossed a mental bridge back when he left London, deciding that career progression came second to having a life. Still some work to do on that front; no woman, no kids, and no social life to speak of yet. Restlessness pulled at his sleeve like an impatient child, after all, the real driving force behind coming back was being closer to Mary.

She left him the house and a surprisingly large cash inheritance. He toyed with just chucking it all in, buggering off around the world. Never going to happen - he was a cop and he'd stay a cop. What else was he going to do? Run a bar? Charter fishing boats? Become a gentleman of leisure? No, it might not be Alloa but he'd be catching bad guys for some time yet. Noticing the small things was one of those skills he'd honed. A small thing broke into his meandering thoughts and brought him into the room again.

"Ian, why is Kirsty drinking orange juice? She driving?"

Barr tapped the side of his nose and leaned in close to Stark. "Shhh. I never told you this, right, but we're going to be a baby."

Despite the drink affecting his delivery, Stark knew what Barr meant. "Bloody hell Ian, that's fantastic news!"

"Shhh, for fuck's sake, sir. If she finds out I've told you, she'll bloody kill me."

"Aye, I bloody will kill you, Ian Barr, big mouth."

Barr nearly took a coronary then all three of them laughed. Stark pecked Kirsty on the cheek and shook Barr's hand.

Stark grabbed a bottle of beer, Barr looking at him askance as he did so.

"Here's to Mary and here's to new beginnings."

His new friends toasted with him and oh, man, the beer tasted good. Too good.

***

Billy McDuff feared no-one. Confidence was all it took, showing weakness would bring you all the grief you could ever want but swagger, indifference and a cool head would always see you right in prison. Ten years was a substantial stretch. If you added the previous twenty odd years to that pile, it was far longer than he was prepared to put up with. It was time.

Visiting time; the same zoo, the same collection of caged animals desperate for attention. The chairs uncomfortable, plastic, designed for the arse of a supermodel on hunger strike. The babble incessant, irksome. He'd grown accustomed to quiet, to time alone in contemplation. Large gatherings were unwelcome.

"Hello, son."

"Hiya, Da. How's it going?"

"Oh, you know, alright. How's things wi' you?"

"Aye, no' bad, eh."

Stilted, awkward, limited communication, unaltered by the circumstances; they'd always talked to each other like this.

"How's Jack?"

"Em, aye, he's ok."

"Still doing alright at the fitba?"

"I think so, aye. I'm no' that sure, Da. Since I moved out I don't see them much, you ken?"

Billy nodded. Turning sixteen allowed Cammy to move out the house, his mother paying for a flat in Stirling. It was surely only imagination but Billy saw a harder edge, a much older boy than the one who visited a few weeks ago. It encouraged him.

"Cammy, I need you to do something for me."

"Aye, what?"

"I want you to sort him out."

"Who?"

"You ken who. I have to be careful here. Grasses, cameras, microphones everywhere. You ken who I mean."

Cammy clasped his hands, forearms resting on his knees, head dropped to inspect the tiled floor.

"I don't care how you do it, I don't care how long it takes, but I want him sorted, right?"

Cammy looked up. He knew who his Da meant and he wanted him sorted too.

"Ok, I'll sort it, Da. It's going to take a bit of organising but I'll let you know. It's no' going to be easy though."

"No, I ken that, son. Take as long as you need to get it done right. Don't take any big risks, use your Ma's money. I'll start asking about in here. Bound to be someone who can help."

"Ok, Da, I've got to go. I'll be back in touch. I'll sort it though. I promise."

Thank You!

Thank you for buying this book - I really hope you enjoyed it. If you did, it would be great if you could leave a review on Amazon.

You can visit my website at *petercarroll.ravencrestbooks.com*, and while you are there, I'd be delighted if you also subscribed to my blog. That way, I can keep you up to date with future books and other writing adventures.

Look out for my other novels *Stark Contrasts, In Many Ways* and *Pandora's Pitbull* which are all available from Amazon.

All the best

Peter

THE FIRST IN THE ADAM STARK DETECTIVE SERIES

It drives you mad right? All those anti-social behaviours you endure every day in a big city - inconsideration, selfishness, low level violence, intimidation. You wish you had the nerve, the strength of character to intervene, to speak out, to do...something. Well, someone in London has had enough and they are doing something about it.

Something drastic.

As punishments escalate in severity and the press make a champion of this anti-hero, Detective Inspector Adam Stark is desperately trying to make sense of what's going on. Random, unconnected victims, excessive retribution, red herrings, kidnap, mutilation, mistaken identity, gangsters, revenge and murder. Things are getting totally out of hand.

Stark needs to nail this sociopath with a social conscience, but the case might just be running away from him - heading toward a brutal and bloody conclusion.

Thriller of the Month - May 2013 at e-thriller.com

"Entertaining reading and will make you think twice again before tailgating on the roads, spitting gum or playing your music too loud on public transport!"

Rating: Great satisfaction for any reader!

If you have a smart phone, scan the barcode for a link to "Stark Contrasts"

In Many Ways

A young man is abducted and mutilated for talking out of turn, and a policeman is murdered as a result – all in a day's work for Danny O'Neill, Scotland's most notorious gangster.
Meanwhile, small-time drug dealer and shop worker Davie

Argyle has just crossed O'Neill's path. Davie has been waiting a long time for this. He needs to swallow his pride and convince O'Neill to trust him. Thing is, can he stay alive long enough for his plan to work?
Torture, murder, rock n roll and bloody revenge ensue as pasts unfurl and long-held secrets reveal themselves. In many ways, it was only a matter of time until it all kicked off...

Thriller Of The Month on www.e-thriller.com *"...following firmly in the footsteps of the pioneers of 'Tartan Noir' trail blazed by Ian Rankin and his erstwhile detective John Rebus, Peter Carroll takes us away from the prim and proper streets of the capital Edinburgh and takes us instead to the mean streets of Glasgow. Recommended and riveting reading from a relatively new author."*

If you have a smart phone, scan the barcode for a link to "In Many Ways"

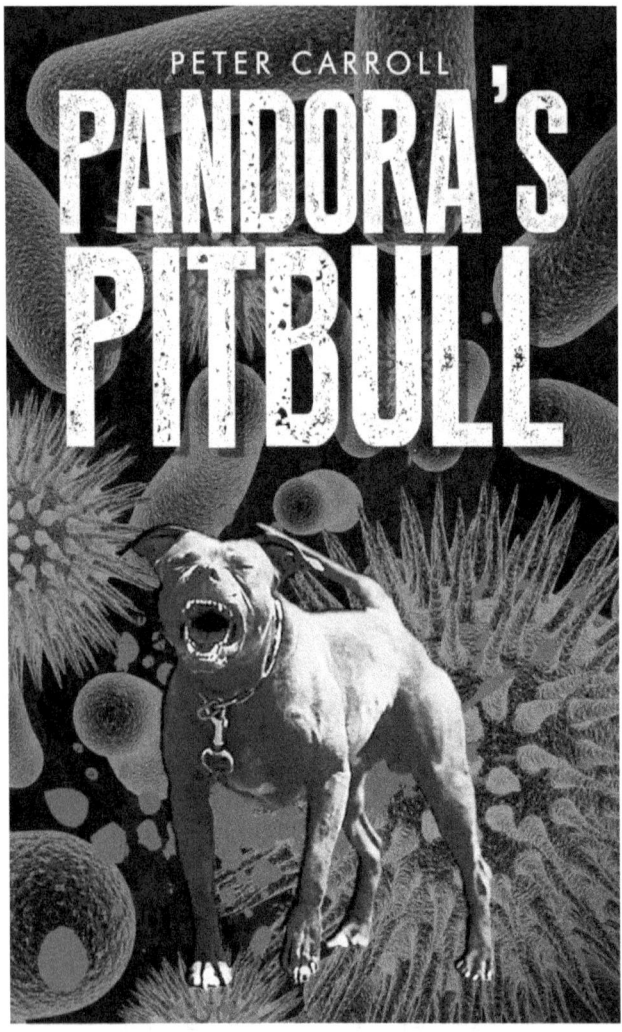

PETER CARROLL

PANDORA'S PITBULL

Two clandestine world's have collided - with disastrous
consequences.

A fighting dog, kidnapped and used in a top secret
experiment, is free and carrying a virus. A virus like

nothing that's gone before. A virus that's spreading through Scotland unchecked.
As society implodes and people refuse to die a normal death, the fates of a small boy, a young woman, a soldier and the very country they live in will hang in the balance.

A new evil has been unleashed on the world but it might be too late to put the lid back on this particular box...
Indie Book of the Month August 2012

"Fantastic book! I absolutely love Carroll's writing style. Carroll is a true talent at writing intelligent and witty material."
RA Stephenson author of "Collapse (New America #1)"

If you have a smart phone, scan the barcode for a link to "Pandora's Pitbull"

About The Author

Peter Carroll is a Scotsman with a penchant for black humour and gritty realism. As well as writing, he's passionate about nature conservation and music.

Peter has four novels under his belt so far: crime thriller "In Many Ways", apocalyptic horror "Pandora's Pitbull", and the Adam Stark detective series, "Stark Contrasts " and "Stark Choices "

"Stark Choices" is his fourth novel.

Contact Details

Visit the authors website:
petercarroll.ravencrestbooks.com

www.twitter.com/petercarroll10

Cover designed by: Raven Crest Books

Published by: Raven Crest Books
www.ravencrestbooks.com

Follow us on Twitter:
www.twitter.com/lyons_dave